MARIA
1843

PRAIRIE ROSES
COLLECTION
BOOK 44

Anna
JENSEN

A note on language: I am a most English author, despite having lived in South Africa for many years; I, therefore, use British English phraseology and spelling rather than American, so please forgive me if anything isn't clear or isn't spelt as you might expect.

First Edition April 30, 2024

ASIN : (ebook) B0CW1QX452
Coming soon in Print.

Cover art by Randi Gammons of Randi Gammons Graphic Design
Branding for series by Chatona Having

TABLE OF CONTENTS

Acknowledgements

Thank you to <u>Caryl McAdoo</u> for encouraging me to join the 2024 Prairie Rose Collection. Without her, the would be no MARIA.

Thank you to the other Prairie Rose authors for welcoming me to their band of happy travellers. I can honestly say I'm honoured to be included amongst your ranks.

To **Randi Gammons,** thank you for creating such a lovely cover and finding the perfect MARIA to grace the cover.

Thanks to friend and fellow author <u>Dianne J Wilson</u> for cheering me on each time MARIA stumbled. Having you in my corner makes a world of difference.

Thank you to another friend and author <u>Vida li Sik</u> for your help in navigating the romance genre – a first for me. Your input was super valuable and help guide MARIA's journey.

To <u>Allyson Koekhoven</u>, friend and editor. Thank you for speedy and helpful editing. I promise I won't cut it so fine next time!

Thank you to **Craig** and **Leal** for covering for me on the days when MARIA took centre stage. And thank you, **Caragh,** for your cheers from a distance!

Thank you, Jesus, for the gift of co-creating stories and worlds with you. What a journey you take me on!

Dedication

To the pioneers and pilgrims; and to all who offer them safe havens

Then they cried to the Lord in their trouble,
and he delivered them from their distress;
he made the storm be still,
and the waves of the sea were hushed.
Then they were glad because they had quiet,
and he brought them to their desired haven.

Psalm 107:28-30 (RSV)

CHAPTER ONE

Graaff-Reinet, South Africa, September 1836

"Ow!" Maria jerked free from under Tannie Johanne's ministrations with the hair clips.

"Stand still, child. Or I'll never finish this plait." A second ferocious poke.

"Maybe I don't want you to finish it. Is all this really necessary? Won't I keep my bonnet on most of the time?" Maria rubbed at her scalp.

"You'll be grateful when you've been on the trail for four or five days without a comb to make yourself tidy." Tannie Johanne swatted the hand away. "There, that should hold for a while. Now, let me look at you."

Maria swivelled around to face her aunt. Brown eyes and a wrinkled forehead scrutinised her in the dim lamplight as though she were a specimen under an inspection glass. The frown smoothed into a smile as Tannie Johanne nodded her approval.

"You will do us proud." The paper dry skin of her fingers whispered over Maria's cheek. "Me and your Ma and…"

Maria interrupted the compliment. She didn't want the reminder, not today. "Why can't you come too? I'm sure Oom Erasmus could make space for you. You could travel in the back of their wagon, I'm certain."

"I'm too old for that life. You know I am. But you?" Tannie Johanne fiddled with the lace collar of Maria's favourite dress. The one the colour of the African sky. Like her eyes, so everyone said. "Oom Erasmus is offering you the opportunity of a lifetime, allowing you to travel with him and his family into a land of great promise. A land the Lord will give to those who are true to His calling and His ways, who resist the ungodly influence of the British settlers."

Tannie Johanne's lips curled upwards, her disdain for the British as obvious as if eating a spoiled morsel of food. Maria suspected she would have spat the taste from her mouth if etiquette in front of her niece had allowed.

"But perhaps I should stay here until they're settled, Tannie. I can wait here as your companion while they establish proper transport routes, start building the towns we shall live in. Wouldn't that be better?" The bedroom curtains rustled in a sudden gust of pre-dawn wind. Shadows loomed and retreated as the lamp's flame spluttered. Tannie Johanne twisted the burner's wick.

Maria shivered in the chill. The memory of another spring dawn huddled in an oversized coat, a hand-knitted shawl wrapped around her chin and neck. Inhaling Ma's perfume on the fabric, the coarseness of its wool itching at her skin. Longing to curl her hand into Pa's grip rather than bury it deep in a pocket dirty from his tobacco. Wishing someone would interrupt the dominee, rush from the morning shadows, explain it was a monstrous mistake, that the service wasn't necessary. Declare to all present that the Steyns weren't the ones being lowered into the gaping earth…

It was a familiar dream. Or nightmare. Maria blinked against the sting of tears she couldn't afford to shed.

Tannie Johanne appeared not to notice. Or pretended, perhaps. "Oom Erasmus sent his servants to collect your trunk yesterday. So, there's only a few things left to pack this morning. I understand you're to reach the first hills at the edge of town before sundown today. Although I'm not sure the oxen are aware of that expectation. They might rebel and decide to pull only as far as the river." She chuckled, a dry, mirthless parody of her usual infectious humour.

"Yes, or Mr Maritz's wagons will be too heavy for them, with everyone's belongings loaded on them." Realising she wasn't the only one struggling with her emotions, Maria joined Tannie Johanne's false lightheartedness.

Tannie Johanne didn't reply, her expression again serious. She reached for Maria's hands, held them in the space between them. Calloused thumbs rubbed Maria's skin in rhythmic circles. Diamond drops glistened on faded eyelashes as her eyelids closed.

"Heavenly Father..." Faltering words spoken from a breaking heart, Tannie Johanne's lips a tight line of determined self-control.

Maria wanted to yank herself free, to run to Oom Erasmus, retrieve her few possessions and shout to anyone listening that she would stay right here in Graaff-Reinet. Where she belonged. Where Ma and Pa...

Somehow sensing the turmoil, Tannie Johanne's grip tightened. "Heavenly Father, we thank you for giving Maria the way to a new life. And for several in this town to be with her as she goes. Thank you for Gert Maritz and his pioneering, voortrekker spirit. Thank you for Erasmus and Susanna as they lead your flock and gather your children under the wing of your protection." The prayer gathered momentum, filled the small room with the flickering lantern and fluttering hearts. Praise entwined with supplication as pleas for health and safety, for discoveries of fresh water and safe havens overflowed from an old woman's devotion. Tension melted from Maria's shoulders, caressed and comforted as she had been from childhood by another's faith and love.

Another's faith. A momentary stab of unease. Whose faith would carry her now? Was God able to journey to pastures new and remain here at the same time? Or would He have to forsake one to keep close to the other? Who would He choose? A dark fog swirled at the edges of her mind. Of course, He would stay with Tannie Johanne.

"Amen." The older woman ended her prayer. Light shone from her opened eyes, sadness dissolved in the assurance of being heard. The fog thickened. Maria missed the blanket of that assurance already.

Tannie Johanne released Maria's hands. With a sigh full of deep contentment, she stepped to the window and swished open the curtains. Shades of delicate pink and orange suffused the room as the rising sun painted the sky. A bird sang a melody of morning greeting. The scent of the dew-refreshed garden wafted in on the breeze.

"You have a fine day for the journey's start. The Lord's smile of blessing, don't you think?"

A shiver tickling along Maria's spine the only response.

"I picked these for you." Tannie Johanne busied herself at the wooden dresser beside the window. Their dishes from last night's supper — washed and dried as soon as they'd eaten the simple meal of stew and bread — clinked as she moved them to the side; gold-rimmed prettiness preserved through decades of travels. "I thought you might take them down to the church before you leave. We're up early — you have time."

Tannie Johanne clutched a collection of blue, yellow and pink flowers, the best of the spring blooms decorating her garden.

Maria stepped back, distancing herself from the posy and all it represented. Her aunt asked too much.

"I know you don't want to. But you'll regret not doing so. They'll want to hear you're leaving. For now."

The flowers blurred and swam in Maria's vision as the threatened tears overflowed and slid down her cheeks. Tannie Johanne, instantly by her side, pulled Maria into her arms, engulfing the sorrow in her embrace. Soft clucking sounds, accompaniment to much of her girlhood, penetrated Maria's sobbing misery.

CHAPTER TWO

Graaff-Reinet, South Africa. September 1836

The oxen dipped their heads, grunts and snorts communicating their displeasure as drivers cajoled them into position between the wagon traces. Boxes and crates passed from hand to hand as servants stowed belongings into the covered wagons, their masters and mistresses shouting conflicting orders and instructions. A three-legged iron cooking pot swung from a pole hefted between two bare-chested men, their dark skin glistening with sweat. Another man jogged past, whistling through his teeth, a cage — out of which protruded the chestnut feathers of a cockerel — swinging at his side.

Children dodged in and out, further increasing the oxen's distress. Someone swatted a couple of giggling, racing boys away with a leather switch. The sjambok split the air with a crack, startling the boys into a sudden stillness. Shock registered in howls of fright as they scuttled off in search of their mamas.

Gert Maritz, supervising the loading of a supply wagon, paused in his labours at the ensuing commotion. He scowled at the assembly, thick brows drawn low over eyes darting from group to group.

"He's getting worried it's taking too long. I know that look." Tannie Johanne squeezed Maria's elbow, steering her around the confusion. "He'll explode in a rage soon, if this chaos continues. Come on, let's make sure we don't contribute to his frustrations. There's Erasmus and Susanna."

Maria tugged the strap of her linen bag further up her shoulder, ducking her head to avoid Meneer Maritz's glance as they passed. Her boots clumped on the winter-hardened surface of the town square, pinching her toes with their unyielding new leather stiffness. Nights of Tannie Johanne bent over her needle and thread in the guttering light of the lantern had allowed for the boots' purchase. According to the seamstress, the extra work was a gift from God, but Maria noticed the struggle to rise from the chair in the morning, the weary slump of the shoulders, the purple circles under the eyes. A gift at the recipient's expense?

Maria quickened her pace, determined the sacrifice would be worth it. She resolved to honour her aunt by serving the Smit family with all her heart, to do whatever they bid of her, to tackle hardship and trials without grumbling or complaining. And when settled in their new land, she would send for Tannie Johanne and bring her to live in a cottage surrounded by roses, and filled with laughter and love.

"Johanne Steyn. And young Maria. Welcome to our home for the next few months." Oom Erasmus strode towards them, hand outstretched and voice booming above the chatter of his wife and sons.

The fog drifted over Maria's vision for the future.

"Thank you, Erasmus." Tannie Johannes face dimpled into a smile. She released her hand from Maria's elbow, transferring it to shake that of her favourite not-really grandson. "I trust we haven't delayed your departure. We needed to pay a visit to — well, someone important — before we came."

A look of understanding exchanged between guardians. Maria had the distinct impression of a responsibility transferring from one to another as the handshake lengthened beyond mere greeting; a parcel delivered, with no say in its destiny.

"Not at all." Oom Erasmus indicated the bustle with a waggle of his free hand and a shake of the head. "I think Gert underestimated how long this would take. It's quite the undertaking, transplanting a whole life. Susanna? Johanne and Maria are here. Won't you get the girl settled?"

Tannie Susanna straightened from the basket she appeared to be sorting. Wiping her hands down a white apron already stained with streaks of grime, she approached Maria with a wide smile and distracted expression in her blue eyes. Curls of dark blond hair escaped from under a bonnet whose strings flapped loose. "Maria, welcome. And Tannie Johanne, it is good to see you." She kissed the older woman on the cheek, dwarfing her in height and bulk. "Erasmus, have you seen George or Saloman? I sent them to enquire as to whose spare oxen we're to utilise today, and I haven't seen them since."

"No, dear, I have not." Impatience tinged Oom Erasmus' reply. "You really should pay closer attention to the pair of them. They may be of adult age, but they are assuredly not of adult temperament."

Twin dots of crimson shame blushed Tannie Susanna's cheeks. Or was it anger? Tension fizzled between husband and wife.

"Now then, Susanna, Maria here is ready to be of service." Tannie Johannes gentle intervention diffused the prickled atmosphere. She placed an age-spotted hand on Maria's arm.

Maria focussed on the hand, committing to memory every snaking vein, every chipped fingernail, the knuckles wrinkled and the joints stiff from the hours of sewing. Oh, how was she to do this alone, without this hand by her side, guiding and leading her into an unimagined future? She bit down on the rising surge of panic and anguish.

"Yes, yes, what am I thinking?" Tannie Susanna placed her own strong, unlined hand on Maria's shoulder. Transaction begun. "Follow me, Maria, and we'll check that we have your belongings stowed safely in the wagon. Then you can perhaps assist with stowing the provisions we have for the next few days — weeks, I hope — of our journey."

Tannie Johannes fingers tightened their grip on Maria for one, eternal, second before releasing their pressure. She buried her hand in the folds of her dress as if scared it might develop a life of its own and cling on to her charge without ever letting go. Or so Maria wanted to believe. Hold on to me forever...

Only Tannie Susanna's hand responded to Maria's heart cries, its weight drawing her away from her aunt. From her home. And from others who would never travel with her.

The church clock erupted into midday chimes, startling Maria with its persistent tolling. The reminder of the marching progression of time galvanised the travellers into action; oxen bellowed as drivers shouted and whistled, fathers jumped onto horses, mothers gathered children and shooed them into the back of laden wagons.

"I must go and counsel Gert to issue orders to depart. We shall barely have journeyed beyond the town's boundary by nightfall, at this rate." Oom Erasmus removed his hat, exposing thinning wisps of hair, and bowed in low farewell before Tannie Johanne. "Goodbye, Tannie Johanne. With the help of God, we shall take good care of Miss Steyn as we journey to the freedom He has for us. I am only sorry you feel unable to accompany us yourself."

"Thank you, Erasmus. Maria is in the right company with you as her benefactor and chaperone. And no, you wouldn't want the burden of an old lady like me with you."

"Come then, Maria. Erasmus is right — we need to attend to our affairs, and with some urgency, if we're to reach the hills this evening." Tannie Susanna gave a gentle tug on the arm she still held. "Child, I'll leave you to your farewells, but please don't be longer than necessary. There is much to do and I'll appreciate your help. Oh. there's George. George! Where have you been? Did you secure a team to pull the wagon…?"

Tannie Susanna abandoned Maria, whirling around, and hurrying after her son.

Alone with Tannie Johanne, in a pool of stillness from the surrounding hustle and bustle, a wave of aloneness made Maria dizzy with its intensity.

"Tannie…" Arms drew her close. Starched cloth muffled her cries, the scent of roses wreathing her grief.

"Ssh. All will be well." The soothing motion between her shoulders. "The Lord has opened the way. He will be with you. As will I, through my prayers and constant thoughts. You'll see, you won't feel as far away as you think."

Maria gulped, swallowing her sorrow. She extricated herself from Tannie Johannes embrace, looked into a face as familiar as her own. She reached to wipe a tear from the wrinkled cheek.

"Thank you, Tannie. You will travel in my heart for always." She straightened, hitched her bag higher on her shoulder. "And I shall write. I shall keep a diary and send you its pages whenever I can."

Tannie Johanne dabbed at her eyes with a handkerchief pulled from her sleeve. She laughed — a tinkle of joy Maria tucked into her treasury of memories. "Perhaps not the whole diary. A few lines will do."

Maria took a deep breath. It was time.

"Goodbye. I love you, Tannie Johanne. With all I am. I…" She couldn't continue. She clenched her jaw, willing herself to move. The boots on her feet felt heavy, clumsy, gluing her to the spot. She forced herself to turn, to drag distance between her and Tannie Johanne.

"And I love you, Maria Steyn." The voice muffled by the engulfing swirl of fog. "Farewell, precious child."

Transaction complete.

CHAPTER THREE

Outside Graaff-Reinet, South Africa. September 1836

Maria waggled her toes in the cooling eddies of the stream. Unfamiliar boots worn from dawn till dusk while tramping over rugged terrain gave rise to blistered heels and swollen ankles. Some of the group's older boys waded into the water, bare-chested, splashing and screaming at the shock of the frigid temperature. Maria laughed as one after another they ducked below the surface, reappearing with grins of bravado, hair dripping and bodies shivering. Their female counterparts, paddling in the shallows alongside Maria, giggled and pointed, declaring their friends and brothers, cowards or heroes, depending on whether they stumbled to the banks or remained swimming.

Maria, after only three days of journeying, already relished such moments — the hours of monotonous trekking behind them, the sun snuggling below the horizon as it spread a cosy blanket of orange and red and pink across the landscape; the oxen released from their traces, lowing in contented freedom as they wandered the veld or chewed on their post-work feed; wagons laagered into their protective circle and smoke rising from the infant campfires.

She rolled the ache from her shoulders, leaning back against a rock. She closed her eyes, inhaling the evening perfumes of wood-smoke and damp vegetation. The cries of the playing children faded into silence as they trotted away to their families and warmth and food. Weaver birds chatted in the branches of a nearby thorn tree, settling themselves in their plaited nests for the night.

Alone. A few precious minutes before Tannie Susanna called Maria to help with meal preparations, or to test the community's children on their letters, or to repack a box of provisions after it jiggled loose during the journey. She wasn't unkind, but the constant demands for assistance grated on Maria. Tannie Johanna kept a neat home, was strict with her discipline and expectations. But there was always space for music or reading or sketching. Sewing could be the mundane chore of darning and mending one day; delicate embroidery the next.

Tannie Susanna demanded every moment be filled with some worthwhile activity. She frowned if Maria pulled a book from the linen shoulder bag, tutted with audible disapproval if the needle and thread traced a pattern of flowers and leaves. And sitting engaged in nothing other than reflection and daydreaming? There should be none of that.

With only the burble of the stream and the call of the birds to chastise her, Maria allowed a parade of images from the day to flit through her mind. From their mid-morning start, the plod towards the grey hulk of the mountain range ahead was the same as ever — the men riding out on horseback, exploring the route, and ensuring safe passage; the women striding out alongside the wagons, toddlers peering from the covered interiors, complaining at the injustice of being forced into the wheeled transport rather than skipping along the path with those older than them.

Maria played games with the young captives, calling out a letter of the alphabet and encouraging them to search for an object within their limited range of vision which began with that letter. When interest waned, she told Tannie Johanna's remembered stories of ships sailing across mighty oceans, and men and women risking their lives to reach the safe harbour of the Cape. These she embellished with fictitious encounters experienced with sea monsters or pirates.

The calm monotony of the morning shattered as the scouts returned in a flurry of hoofbeats and clouds of dust. They galloped to Meneer Maritz's leading wagon, waving their hats, and shouting indistinct warnings. Oom Erasmus, trotting on his horse beside Tannie Susanna, roused himself from a slumped doze, blinking in slow disorientation. Maria suppressed a chuckle at his owl-like appearance. Even his beard ruffled like a bird's tousled feathers.

"I shall ride to Gert, discover what's going on." Oom Erasmus flicked the horse's reins. "Susanna, I suggest you gather the children and either return them to their mothers or stow them, for safety's sake, in our wagon. And then you and Miss Steyn similarly seek refuge within."

Susanna opened her mouth as though about to object. Giving the smallest shake of her head, she clamped her lips over the words — a common occurrence, Maria was discovering.

Oom Erasmus bent forward, his eyes searching his wife's face. For signs of the stubbornness he so often preached against in his Sunday sermons? Or a look of concern and compassion at this unexpected interruption to the routine?

"Yes, dear. Maria and I will do that immediately." Tannie Susanna's response suggested the former. "Please hurry back to us with any news you receive. Maria, let's round up these children. I think it safest to pile them into the back with us and remain with them for the duration of whatever transpires. We can continue with their lessons while we wait."

Satisfied at his wife's obedience, Oom Erasmus galloped away, calling for his sons to accompany him as he rode.

Time dragged in the stuffy confines of the canvas material. The children grew fidgety and restless, fear and uncertainty seeming to travel along the rumbling procession.

"Perhaps we should find them something to eat?" Maria kept her voice a low whisper, not wanting to lift the children's hopes in case Tannie Susanna felt further work on their spelling was required.

"That's an excellent idea." Relief tinged the reply. "There's a crate of apples somewhere. What's taking so long? I expected Erasmus and the boys to have returned by now."

"I'm sure all will be well. Perhaps they've found a better way to pass over the mountains and are discussing the possibilities." Maria, somewhat bewildered at the sudden change in role from helper to comforter, crawled away to search for the apples.

The fruit saved the moment. The children chomped and slurped, Tannie Susanna regained her composure, and Maria savoured the break from teaching. She shuffled to the end of the wagon, dangling her feet over its edge. Her boots swung in rhythmic time with the continued plod of the oxen, the wheels crunching over the dry winter ground with a satisfying solidity. The sun hung golden in the noontime blue of a clear sky. The scents of dust and crushed grass mingled with the aromatic sweetness of the apple Maria munched.

Shouts, the thudding of hooves, a few whistles and cheers, disturbed the sleepy peace.

"Tannie Susanna. They're back." Maria hopped down from the wooden tailgate as Tannie Susanna shuffled forward, blinking in the sunlight.

"Is Erasmus with them? The sun's in my eyes. I can't see a thing."

"Yes, he is. Oom Erasmus. George, Saloman. What news?" In her eagerness for information, Maria forgot her customary deference. George's eyes widened in evident surprise. "Sorry, where are my manners? Tannie Susanna is with the children in the wagon. I can convey your messages to her, if you wish."

"Tell Susanna to prepare for company." Oom Erasmus sat tall in his saddle. His eyes glittered with excitement, the boredom of earlier chased away by whatever tidings he carried. A flutter of anxiety registered deep in Maria's consciousness. A wisp of fog clouding her contentment. Company? What company? "Andries Pretorius and his men are joining us. Isn't that wonderful?"

"Pretorius? What does he want with us? Has he come to recruit more boys into his commando?" Suspicion oozed from Susanna's inquiry. The contrast between Oom Erasmus's delight and Tannie Susanna's disapproval confused Maria. She held her tongue.

"Susanna. do you always have to jump to the worst conclusion? The Lord has sought fit to bring companions to our side, able men willing to aid us with our passage through the mountains. We are few, and unlikely to navigate the treacherous slopes and gorges without assistance. Their arrival is the hand of Providence."

"Erasmus, that is unfair of you…"

A sharp crack of a breaking twig close by banished further recollection of the confrontation between husband and wife. Maria snapped her eyes open, snatching her feet from the stream as though its waters suddenly boiled with scalding ferocity. She curled her knees to her chin, her arms wrapped tight around her shins and her heart pounding. She bit down on the fabric of her apron, willing herself not to cry out.

Something — or someone — approached through the shadowed gloom.

CHAPTER FOUR

Outside Graaff-Reinet, South Africa. September 1836

A lilting whistle. A person then; not an animal.

Maria spat the apron from between her teeth at the relief of knowing a prowling leopard wasn't about to tear her limb from limb. Her panicked breathing eased. How Tannie Johanne would tease her. If she were here…

It was probably one of the wagon drivers collecting water for his animals. Sighing at the thought of tugging boots onto her blistered feet, Maria scrambled down the bank to retrieve the offending articles. Then froze, her heart jumping from her chest into her mouth.

A figure stepped from the lengthening shadows of the thorn trees. A man — and not a wagon driver.

The intruder approached the riverbank, shrugging out of a dark blue jacket as he walked. Dumping the overcoat in a heap, he rolled up the sleeves of his grubby white shirt. As he bent to remove his battered-looking boots, something caught his attention.

Maria.

A whimpering sound rose in her throat and escaped her lips. This wasn't George or Saloman, or any of their friends. This was a stranger unknown to her. And she was alone, further than screaming distance from her guardians and protectors.

The man hurried upright, his face contorted with shock. Or animosity? A scraggy beard hugged his chin, while curly brown hair looked squashed and hat-weary. Brown eyes widened as Maria, torn between curling into the smallest, most insignificant ball she could manage, or scrambling to her feet to confront the newcomer, found her muscles unable to perform either option, and instead burst into tears.

"Please, no, don't cry." The man raised his palms. "I'm so sorry I startled you. I didn't know anyone was here."

He advanced a step. Maria's body dissolved into shivers as she recoiled from his approach. She reined in the tears, gulping them away with determined swallows. She chewed on her apron fabric once more.

He paused.

"Look, I can leave. Return to the camp. But at least allow me to introduce myself before I go."

At the prospect of his departing, Maria relaxed. She could wait for him to say his piece, then watch as he strode away. Once assured he was no longer lurking anywhere close by, she would unravel herself, stuff her feet into her boots and run like the wind to Oom Erasmus and Tannie Susanna. A second possibility dawned on her as the sun took its final bow behind the silhouetted mountainous horizon; they might soon send out a search party for her.

Imagining the consternation that would cause, the look on Oom Erasmus' livid face, Tannie Susanna's disappointment and disapproval blanketing her for the rest of their travels, determined her response to the man. She would allow him his introduction, then hurry behind him to the laager.

The man stood watching her, his head cocked to one side, a hint of a smile fidgeting his beard. Tannie Johanne always said Maria's face told a greater story than her words ever would; he'd read her reasoning as easily as a book, hadn't he? With a huff of irritation at her traitorous features, Maria lifted her chin and waited.

The man settled his features into a serious expression. He folded at the waist in a formal bow of introduction. "I am Field-Cornet Christiaan Venter. I ride with Commandant Andries Pretorius and his commando." He straightened. "We stumbled across some of your men this morning, and agreed to escort your party through the mountains. We have travelled much throughout this area, and are familiar with the terrain and its difficulties. I came to the river to refresh myself after our day's riding, little thinking anyone would still be here at such a late hour of the day. Once again, I apologise for startling you."

Throughout his speech, Maria watched for any indication of his teasing or threatening her. Something about him reminded her of Tannie Johanne. Perhaps it was the same-colour hair, or the lilt of his accent. She couldn't quite put her finger on it. But whatever it was, her muscles released their frightened tension and her breath filled her lungs rather than catching in her chest.

"Would you mind if I stepped closer? I would be happy to leave, as I said, but it is getting dark and I think it may be better if I accompany you and restore you to your family." He hesitated. "I presume you are journeying with the group we have joined for the next few days? I don't see any farmhouses or other dwellings nearby?"

Maria tugged the soggy apron from her mouth. Deep shadows blurred the outline of the opposite bank of the stream, a chill dampness swirling above its waters. Maybe someone accompanying her to camp wasn't such a bad idea. She unwrapped her arms from around her knees, stretching her legs in front of her. Pins and needles tingled in her foot.

"Ow." She stood, only to collapse back to the ground as her sleeping foot refused to bear weight.

Two loping strides and Christiaan was at her side. "Let me help you up. It's my fault you're all tangled up like that. And you must be feeling cold." Maria's chattering teeth had less to do with the temperature than the fresh wave of panic engulfing her. The proximity of the man, his bulk hovering over her, his eyes searching her face…that was it, the eyes. That's what brought Tannie Johanne to mind. They were kind eyes. And on closer inspection, he was nearer her own age than she'd first thought.

"Thank you." Shoving her fear aside, realising at this stage she had no choice but to accept his offer of assistance, she held out her hand. Christiaan grabbed it, hauling her upright. She leant against him, balancing on one leg while shaking the other, her circulation returning with a pulsing throb. Eager to hang onto the man for as short a time as possible, she ignored the discomfort in her reawakening limb and regained her balance. "I'm fine now. I'll just put my boots on."

"I'll help. If you sit down, we might not get you up again. Lean on me so you don't fall over." Laughter crinkled his nose. Another similarity to Tannie Johanne. Christiaan knelt in the damp grass, easing first one foot into a boot, then the other. A peculiar sensation rippled through Maria as he hurried to tie her laces. Her fingers twitched, almost reaching to unfurl the tousled curls bent over her. She snatched her hand away, gripping the folds of her skirt in embarrassed horror. What was she thinking?

She shuffled her booted feet away from Christiaan's attention. He sat back, his hands resting on his thighs. "There. You chose a pretty spot to rest. Listen, isn't that a nightjar?" The bird in question repeated its distinctive warble. "My favourite night-time song. That, and the owl. The creepiest sound is by far the shout of an approaching hyena. Have you heard one yet, um, you didn't tell me your name?"

"Goodness, where are my manners? Tannie Johanne would be appalled." Maria bobbed a half-curtsey, spreading her skirt. "Maria. Maria Steyn. Of Graaff-Reinet."

"Pleased to meet you, Maria Steyn." Christiaan rose, wiping a hand on his trousers before offering it to her in formal greeting. "Tannie Johanne. Is that who you travel with?"

"No, no, I'm with Oom Erasmus and Tannie Susanna. They kindly offered me a place in their wagon in exchange for help with Tannie Susanna's duties." She concentrated on keeping her facial muscles from again betraying her inner thoughts to this stranger. "Tannie Johanne is — she has remained in Graaff-Reinet."

She blinked away the prickles obscuring her vision. Familiar dark clouds fogged her thinking. A gnawing weariness consumed her. She needed to eat more than the apple she'd half-finished earlier, but campfires and cooking pots were a mile or more distant. Perhaps she could flop on the grass, settle on the soft earth and lie up against the heat of the rock, waiting for her strength to recover. Oom Erasmus would send George to look for her on his horse. Tannie Susanna would exclaim over her return, fussing and ensuring they propped her beside the comfort of the fire, while spooning ladles of aromatic vegetables into a bowl.

Her legs crumpled beneath her, the idyllic homecoming evaporating in a gasp of reality — George wasn't coming, only a smouldering fire would greet her arrival, Tannie Susanna impatient for her to start cooking the stew of which she dreamt.

"Oh no, you don't." An arm circled her waist. Those brown eyes, etched with concern and compassion, flicked over her face. Reading the unspoken words. "Here, take my overcoat. You're shivering again."

Christiaan draped the coat over her shoulders, after retrieving it from where he'd dumped it without Maria noticing. It smelt of damp and horse, and there was a faint tang of something like when George and Saloman sat too near to her. With his free hand, Christiaan dug into the front pocket.

"Here, biltong. It's not much, but it'll help until you get a proper meal inside you." He offered the dried meat stick to Maria. She thought she could make out bits of cotton fluff sticking to it. Uncaring and unable to stop herself, she grabbed it from him.

"Thank you." She spoke around a mouthful of salted venison. "I didn't realise how late it was. Nor how long since I've eaten. I'm ready now. Shall we go?"

She shook off his arm, and without a backward glance, swished through the grass towards home. A chuckle as discernible as the bird's continued call followed her progress.

CHAPTER FIVE

Sneeuwbergen Mountains, South Africa. September 1836

"Have you really heard a hyena? Oof, this peg is stuck."
Maria banged the hammer against the wooden peg in another
vain attempt at knocking it from its position. "Do we have to
dismantle every wagon before we go over the mountains?
They don't appear so steep."

"Here, let me try." Christiaan nudged her to one side,
grabbing the mallet before Maria could aim another swing at
the unfortunate peg. "You're getting the angle wrong. It'll
never come loose like that. See?"

He gave the peg a gentle knock, then prised it free with his
thumb and forefinger. He waggled it under Maria's nose; the
triumph of a dentist extracting a difficult tooth.

"Give me that." Maria stretched for the peg dangling just
beyond her reach, even on tiptoe. "Oom Erasmus will be
furious if I lose any of these tiny wagon parts. Oh, that's not
fair."

Christiaan jumped up on the wagon's wheel, delight at his
game flushing his cheeks.

"Careful, or you might topple from your perch." Maria
bumped against him, her shoulder connecting with his leg. He
tumbled to the ground, landing in a laughing heap at her feet.

"I don't know about me not playing fair." He offered the
peg, snatched it away, handed it back. "Your prize, my lady."

Maria's retort died on her lips as Tannie Susanna rounded
the edge of the wagon, surveying and assessing the scene
before her. Her cheeks pinched inward, as though sucking on
an unripe lemon.

"Maria, what do you think you're doing? And Field-Cornet Venter, you surely have somewhere more useful to be than lounging on the grass while the rest of us labour at these preparations for our mountain journey?"

"Yes, sorry. I was helping Maria — Miss Steyn — release the peg on this connector here." Christiaan scrambled to his feet, removing his hat, and attempting a bow of respectful repentance at the same time. "I'll return to my commando now, and my work there. Until later, Miss Steyn. And you're right. The hills don't seem steep from this side, but once we get beyond the foothills, you'll understand the necessity for your efforts."

Was that a wink? Or had some dust, or a fly, blown into his eye?

"Please call on me should you need any more help, especially once the climb gets underway. The terrain is rough and the weather changes in an instant. Your servants will have their work cut out guiding the oxen along the path. I have no such encumbrance and so am at your service."

Tannie Susanna's cheeks relaxed their acidity as Christiaan finished his speech with a second bow. "Thank you, young man, I shall bear that in mind. Now, be off with you. Maria and I have much to do." The sourness returned as Tannie Susanna faced Maria. She held her hand out, palm upward. "I'll take care of that peg. And any others you have. If they go missing, we're in trouble."

Maria handed over the wedge of wood. Christiaan retreated to a safe distance, then removed his hat, waving it in vigorous farewell. Maria swallowed a giggle, her heart lightened by this sudden, unexpected friendship of a mere two days.

Christiaan was right. The hills were steeper up close than from the comforting distance of the valley. Maria moved aside, out of the way of her climbing companions. She licked dry lips with a thick tongue. Sweat trickled down her back where the basket, looped over her shoulders with leather straps, rubbed against her blouse. Someone had surely been adding rocks to her burden on the ascent; its weight dragged and chafed, unlike at the start of the trek.

The men were lucky. They had horses to carry them and their possessions. The snaking trail of puffing, red-faced women and children with Maria were themselves the beasts of burden. Laden with makeshift bags or woven baskets, they toiled upward, one aching step in front of the next.

A gap opened between the women at the point where the path was steepest, below Maria's resting place. An older woman, a plait of grey hair dangling from under her bonnet, plodded in lonely isolation, seeming to prefer to maintain her steady pace rather than the stop-start progress of the others. Her ill-fitting shoes looked as dusty and careworn as her face. Her lips moved as if in private conversation with someone. Whether praying or complaining, Maria couldn't hear.

Without warning, the woman stumbled as her toe caught in a loose stone. Dropping the small box she carried, she tried to steady herself against a scrubby tree growing alongside the track. A length of rope fell from the box, tumbling down the mountainside. The woman, grabbing the branches, cried out in pain. Thorns.

"Tannie. Wait, I'm coming." Unhitching the straps of her basket, Maria wedged her cargo against a rock; she didn't want more supplies to roll away. Taking small, careful steps, she slid to the woman's side. "Take my arm. Here, we'll sit on that rock while you catch your breath. And let me check your hand. That must be painful."

The woman allowed Maria to manoeuvre her to the rock in question. She lowered herself onto the rock; Maria imagined she heard the creak of her protesting bones. "Thank you, child. I'll be all right in a moment. The shock, that's all..." She uncurled her hand, examining a slash of blood across the middle of her palm. "Now look what I've done. So silly. I know the trees in this area are full of thorns. Why did I think I could grab at one and not have it bite me?"

"I'm not sure you had time to think of anything, Tannie. You slipped. Rather you scratch your hand than damage a knee." Maria delved into her apron pocket in search of a rag she could use as a temporary bandage until those better equipped reached them. Her fingers folded around something lacy and soft. Tannie Johanne's handkerchief. The one with her initials embroidered in the corner in tiny, exquisite needlework. A flash of recollection. She'd pushed it into Maria's hand in the churchyard, its whimsical comfort replacing the flower posy she'd lain beside a wooden grave marker.

Maria doubled over, winded by the unbidden reminder of home. Alarm sprang into the older woman's eyes.

"Child, you have over-exerted yourself by helping an absent-minded fool like me. Here, sit beside me, and together we shall rest." She shuffled over, patting the exposed surface of the rock beside her. "You are young to be undertaking this journey alone. Do you not have family accompanying you?"

Her throat too strangled to speak the words of reassurance she ought to utter, Maria groped for the offered seat. A hand settled between her shoulders, rubbing in a familiar pattern of comforting circles. She focused on the sensation, picturing herself in Tannie Johanne's cottage, a child tucked up under a crocheted blanket, reassured by another's gentle touch.

Her breathing slowed, her heart resuming its regular beating. She straightened, reaching for the hand of her companion and holding it in her lap. "My Tannie Johanne does that." She blinked. "Did that. I had to leave her behind. She said she was too old for the trek. I'm sorry, I don't know what came over me. I'm supposed to be helping you, not the other way around."

She attempted a chuckle, making light of her awkwardness.

She risked a glance at the woman. Pale blue eyes held her gaze. The lines and grooves of age patterned the woman's face, telling a story of trial and love and loss and acceptance. Here was another whose heart etched its tale in flesh.

"Tannie Johanne? You are Johanne Steyn's child?" A laugh gurgled in the woman's throat, the creases in her face folding and deepening with obvious joy and delight. "She told me you were coming. Asked me to keep an eye out for you. But everything was such a rush, with Gert impatient to be on the road before I had any opportunity to ask her more about you. She hadn't even told me what you look like. But I see she didn't need to. You are the exact likeness of your mother, when she was your age."

Maria shook her head, trying to create some sort of order out of the chaos the woman's words created.

"Oh, there I go again. A silly old woman jumping ahead of myself and thinking you can read my mind." She extricated her hand from Maria's lap. "I am your Tannie Johanne's friend. Margarite. I'm not from Graaff-Reinet, which is why we've never met. But Gert insisted I travel the extra day or two to reach you all and then continue with his party of intrepid explorers."

"Gert? Oom Gert?" Maria felt like a paper boat adrift on a river in full, mid-summer flood.

"Yes, yes. Gert is my nephew. Did Johanne never speak of me? How remiss of her." She patted Maria's arm. "But then, why would she? We're friends from the olden days, before they established the settlement at Graaff-Reinet. I stayed on the family farm, but she left with your mother's family. A kind of companion for your mother, I suppose. We write, but I don't know that the letters always get through."

"You know Tannie Johanne?" Wide-eyed, Maria searched the woman's face for any sign of falsehood or teasing. She couldn't recall mention of a Margarite. Nor seen any letters with her name signed below. Maria's mind whirled through all the possibilities — the two weren't the close friends Margarite claimed; the woman told the truth, but Tannie Johanne hadn't known of her presence here; or Tannie Johanne knew and had written to her friend, but chosen not to mention anything. Assuming the latter were correct, why would Tannie Johanne not say something, tell Maria of a connection from the old days?

A gasp, as if doused in ice cold water. Hadn't Margarite said something about her looking like Ma? So..."You knew my mother?"

CHAPTER SIX

Sneeuwbergen Mountains, South Africa. September 1836

Margarite's eyes crinkled into sympathy and understanding. "I did. When she was young. About the age you are now, I imagine."

"Fifteen." The automatic reply retrieved from a tangle of disconnected thoughts, lurching emotions.

"Perhaps that's why Johanne didn't say anything. She didn't want to stir up…"

A blast of rage-filled wind blew the advancing fog from Maria's consciousness. "Stir up? How could keeping a secret not stir up more than telling me?" She pulled herself free from Margarite, struggling to disentangle her skirts and scramble off the rock where she sat. "What did she think I'd do if I knew about you? I can talk about them, you know, without — without — "

She stumbled onto the path, tears boiling over and sliding down her face.

"Maria, child. I'm sorry, I should have been more careful. I was so surprised to meet you, I let my delight run ahead of my sense."

The apology added a stab of guilt to the roiling mix of darkness threatening to consume Maria.

"Margarite, dearest, are you alright? What happened?" The scuffle of feet. Chattering voices, alarmed cries. Three women rounded a corner and advanced towards them.

"Hello Magdalena, Aletta. I'm perfectly fine. Just a slight slip and a scratch."

The women surged towards Margarite, fussing, and examining her hand, stroking her arm. Narrowed eyes flicked between their patient and Maria, lips narrowed in judgement and disapproval. The outsider dumped on the pastor. As if his flock weren't already big enough. She'd heard the mutterings around camp. The backs turned, excluding her from their circle of helpful intimacy.

Maria stumbled away. Retrieving her basket, she slung the leather straps over her shoulders, settling the burden on her back — and a weight in her heart.

As the climb grew steeper, the view below stretched out in a mottled pattern of watered farmland and brown, pre-rain fields. The stream near their previous campground threaded through the valley, glistening in the relentless spring sunshine. Trees clustered along its banks. Pausing to sip at the bottle of water stowed in the basket, Maria sought the flickering shade of a clump of mimosa bushes. Careful not to catch her dress on its thorns, she wriggled amongst them, out of the direct glare of the sun.

The conversation with Margarite replayed over and over, joined by disjointed snatches of overheard conversation from Tannie Johanne's parlour. A man in a sombre dark suit and a hat he fiddled with on his lap throughout his stay, mentioning a farm and a right of ownership. Another day, the washed linen flapping in the breeze of a summer's day, and the postman arriving at the gate. Tannie Johanne whispering her thanks, tucking a letter in her apron pocket. Was that from Margarite? Was it her farm the man spoke of before?

The warmth of the afternoon sapped Maria's energy. Her eyelids grew heavy, and a listless stupor settled in her muscles. She curled on her side and allowed the wave of sleepiness to carry her far from the confused turmoil of her memories.

By the time she woke, the shadows from the bushes had retreated and she lay exposed to the sun's rays. But now their heat was a gentle caress, nudging her to wakefulness and urging her to complete her journey before the day stretched into evening. A bee buzzed in and out of the yellow mimosa flowers. A coucal announced the possibility of rain with its warning cry.

Maria shook off the remaining delicious stillness of sleep, then clambered to the track.

For I know the plans I have for you, says the Lord, plans for welfare and not for evil, to give you a future and a hope.

The verse of scripture floated into Maria's mind as she continued upward. She'd spent hours stitching it onto a piece of fine linen under Tannie Johanne's gentle instruction. It hung, framed, in pride of place over Tannie Johanne's bed. The letter P was crooked. Tannie Johanne said perfection was always more beautiful when accompanied by a flaw. Maria hadn't quite believed her, but the thought had made her feel better.

She hauled herself over a pile of rocks, creating a series of natural steps. Her legs ached and the blisters on her feet protested, but the nap had revived her. Her water bottle was empty, but surely it wouldn't be much further. Perhaps the wisp of cloud hovering over the hill's summit was smoke drifting up from the campsite. Maria's mouth watered as she dipped an imaginary spoon into a pretend pot of steaming vegetables. Laughing out loud at her dramatics, she pulled on the straps of the basket and hurried on.

"Watch out. Give the beasts some room!"

Chaos greeted Maria's exhausted trudge into camp. It was like departure day all over again, with boxes and crates piled in haphazard confusion everywhere she looked. Only now, the excited energy of the Graaff-Reinet square no longer fizzled across the camp. Oxen stood with heads lowered, flies buzzing in their noses and ears. They swished their tails and stamped at the ground as servants offloaded the burdens from their backs. Chickens squawked in an improvised coup wedged into the branches of a convenient tree. A dog skipped and barked below them; his frustration clear as they remained beyond his reach.

A group of men huddled around a wagon's reassembled carcass, arms folded and heads nodding. One lifted his hat to scratch an ear. Away to one side, women sat on misshapen bundles of clothes or blankets, children nestled in their laps or curled at their feet. A girl with hair clinging in damp curls on her forehead let out a wail of disapproval as her mother shifted her position.

Maria lowered the basket from her shoulders. She rubbed where the straps had been, certain her skin was chafed raw and her dress spotted with blood. She scanned the different groups, searching for Tannie Susanna or Oom Erasmus. Or even Oom Gert. Where were they? A flutter of disquiet. They were first on the trail as the sun warmed the eastern sky; the leaders preparing their way for the flock to follow.

"Come with us, Maria." Tannie Susanna perched on a borrowed pony. "We can make space…"

"No, we can't, Susanna. The girl will need to make her own way." Oom Erasmus interrupted with firm authority. "There are plenty of women who can chaperone her, should she feel the need. But I'm sure she is more than capable of following a well-worn path in the company of others. After all, they aren't strangers, but kinsfolk from her place of birth."

Tannie Susanna bent her head towards Maria. She spoke in low tones, glancing at Oom Erasmus as he issued instructions to anyone close enough to listen. "Are you sure you will be alright? I promised Tannie Johanne I would take care of you. And here I am, at the first hint of difficulty, leaving you to fend for yourself. I will never forgive myself if something happens to you."

Giddy relief skipped at Maria's heart. Alone at last. Time to observe and ponder. Even sketch a flower or compose her first letter to Tannie Johanne. She hoped Tannie Susanna wouldn't notice the delight shining in her expressive eyes. "No, Tannie, you are needed with Oom Gert and Oom Erasmus. The people will all be looking to you for guidance and reassurance. I can see the route we're to travel, and I'll be sure not to lag behind."

Searching the bustle, that decision now seemed foolish. Oom Erasmus was wrong not to include her in the leading party. How would she ever find them?

Whooping cries broke out behind her as a dozen men galloped into camp, dust billowing around them. Sleeping children woke in startled shock, crying and hugging their mother's necks for comfort. The oxen swung their heads to investigate the noise. A cry of pain and shouts of alarm as a horn pierced the flesh of an unfortunate bystander. The dog abandoned its pursuit of the chickens and raced, teeth bared, towards the newcomers. He collided with a wayward hoof and retreated, whimpering.

At the centre of the raucous group, one rider sat in apparent command. George. His hat dangled between his shoulders from a string around his neck. Sweat dampened his hair and shimmered on his forehead. The buttons of his shirt were loose to the waist and his rolled sleeves exposed sunburnt forearms. He surveyed the crowd as a king his subjects, seeking his prize.

His eyes alighted on Maria. "Ah ha, there you are, cousin of mine. Or whatever you are." He turned to his companions, amused by the jibe. They laughed their approval. "Ma sent me to find you, to scoop you up and return you to her."

He flicked the pony's reins, trotting over to Maria. She stood rooted to the spot, her palms clammy with nerves and embarrassment. All eyes watched her, everything stilled by the performance.

George bent forward; his hand outstretched. Out of view of his fellow riders, he beckoned Maria to him. "Come. Ma is worried about you. I'm sorry, I didn't intend to make a fool of you. My friends sometimes…" He bit his lip. "Hop up here and I'll take you to her. Leave your basket. I'll send someone to fetch it. You look wiped out, you poor thing. We shouldn't have left you, not today. I promise I won't harm you. But I will pretend you're a nuisance. It's only for show. I'm relieved I found you."

The unexpected kindness melted the last of Maria's strength for the day. She gripped the hand, allowing herself to be dragged into the safety of George's arms. She flopped against his shoulder, her head nodding to the rhythm of the horse's trot.

CHAPTER SEVEN

Klein Karoo, South Africa. October, 1836

"Let me help with that, Debora." Maria prised the needles and knitted square of yellow wool from the five-year-old's white-knuckled grip. "You've dropped a couple of stitches here, haven't you? Oh, and added a few somewhere else by the looks of it."

She held up the misshapen rows, wiggling her finger through the largest of the holes. Debora giggled.

"Let's see if we can fix this." Maria slipped the stitches from the needle and pulled on the yarn, undoing rows of Debora's inexpert work. Not to the first two or three rows she'd knitted to start the child off, though; poor Debora would never knit again if she saw her labours unravel before her eyes. But there was no rescuing the final few rows. "There. Now, let's try again. Come here and I'll guide you."

Debora snuggled in close to the circle made by Maria's arms and the knitting. Maria placed the needles in the child's dimpled hands, then held her own over them. This needed more than verbal instructions.

"Don't squeeze the needles so tightly. Imagine you're holding a baby chick. There, that's better." The girl giggled again, then took a deep breath. She bent her golden head over the needles, her tongue sticking out in concentration. "Right, so push the needle through that stitch there. Yes, very good. Next, wrap your wool around — no, not both needles — yes, that's right. Don't pull the wool. It'll make it too hard to get the needle out. That's it. Twist your other needle a bit so you can push it down through that loop. That's it. Well done. And

— carefully — there. You've made a stitch. Let's do that again, only I won't tell you what to do this time."

The wool squeaked along the needles as stitch after labourious stitch formed. After a row and a half of silent concentration, Debora yawned.

"Can I stop now, Tannie Maria? I'm tired. And my fingers ache." Not quite a whine, but almost.

"Yes, I think we've done enough for today. I'll finish this last row for you, then put everything in your basket for next time."

Debora released the needles into Maria's care, wriggling free from her arms. She turned to face her tutor. "Thank you, Tannie Maria." Reaching up, she placed sticky fingers on Maria's cheeks and leant forward, planting a wet kiss on Maria's lips. "I'll see you tomorrow."

The child skipped away. Maria rested the knitting in her lap, taking a moment to savour the sensation of warm belonging Debora's kisses always left her with. It would evaporate like morning dew on a summer's day, but it was precious while it lasted.

"You're very patient with the little ones." A man-boy's voice startled Maria. Her stomach flipped a somersault. Christiaan.

He dropped beside her. He pushed floppy brown curls from his face, ran his hand over a thickening beard. "Sorry, I always seem to make you jump. You were so absorbed with that knitting or whatever it was, I didn't like to interrupt."

Maria shifted her legs to create space on the blanket she'd lain over the stubby grass for herself and Debora. Shade from the wagon behind her offered respite from the burn of the sun. Summer chasing winter off the upper plains with sudden intensity.

"She's a sweet girl. Not very good at knitting, though." She displayed the crooked handiwork. Even with help, the stitches were uneven. "You look hot."

Christiaan wafted his hat in front of his face. "I am. We've been out riding all day. Pretorius wants to scout out the route ahead, find any of the other groups taking the journey north."

"There are others?" Besides Andries Pretorious and his commando, Maria hadn't seen or heard of anyone else navigating the deserted wilderness they travelled. A growing niggle of doubt kept her counting stars for long hours of each night after their successful journey through the hills surrounding Graaff-Reinet. The vast emptiness of the desolate landscape didn't lend itself to the dream of a land of provision and promise, as thumped out by Oom Erasmus in his Sunday sermons. "Even if there are, I don't know how we'd ever meet them. We're like ants on the moon up here."

She shivered. A cloud must have blotted out the sun. She squinted from under her bonnet. No clouds. Only her fear, then.

"Maria, have you never been beyond the boundary of your town?" Christiaan sat straighter, fixed her with his Tannie Johanne eyes of intense scrutiny.

"No. Why would I have?" Maria busied herself with winding up Debora's yarn.

"No need to bite off my head. I remember how small I felt, the first time I came up here. As a boy. I thought the weight of the sky would squash me. I'd never seen anywhere so big or so empty. I couldn't wait to return to the farm." His fingers danced a jig on the rug.

Maria shoved the knitting into the basket at her side, pretended to tidy its contents with careful concentration. If she looked at him, she knew he'd read her thumping heart at the truth of his words. She wanted home, with its streets and houses and gardens of pretty flowers and growing vegetables. She wanted a chair and a table and a bed. And Tannie Johanne bringing her morning coffee and rusks, perching on the bed while they chatted about their plans for the day. The knitting blurred, the colours of the wool mingling into a rainbow of her misery.

"You'll get used to it, I promise. Soon you'll see the beauty of all this." A sweep of an arm, a hand brushing against her shoulder. "You know that bit in the Scriptures where the spies went to explore the new land? And most of them came back and said that giants were there? They told Moses and the people that they'd never be able to take the land, that they were too small and insignificant. Like grasshoppers."

Maria sniffed, the threatened tears drying with the surprise of Christiaan preaching to her. Although it didn't sound like a sermon. More a fireside story, wrapping her in his enthusiasm.

"But two of them disagreed — Caleb and Joshua. They believed God would go with them and they'd be victorious, no matter the odds."

He stopped. Was that the end? Maria risked a quick glance. He rested on his elbows, gazing at the distant horizon as though he'd forgotten her presence.

"I want to be like Joshua. To believe it's possible." He spoke more to himself than to her.

His confession jolted Maria. Joshua had been one of her favourite people in the Bible since a young girl when they'd first read about him in Sunday School. She'd marvelled at his bravery, been awed by his faith in God. She'd never expected to meet a Joshua in real life.

"Anyway, I should go to the others." Christiaan jumped up, dusting grass from his hands. "I'm glad I saw you."

"I'm glad too." Maria tugged on her plait. "I — um — oh, never mind."

"What?" Christiaan bobbed on his heels again. "What were you going to say?"

Maria swallowed. "It's nothing. Really. It's just, well, it's my birthday tomorrow." A hurried rush of words.

"Is it now? Well, we'll have to celebrate, won't we?" Christiaan stood. He grabbed her hands and helped her to her feet. "I'll be sure I find you tomorrow, then."

# CHAPTER EIGHT

Klein Karoo, South Africa. October 1836

Maria twisted the fabric between her hands, the water oozing from its folds. Satisfied George's shirt was as dry as she could make it, she unfolded the bundle and shook out the many creases. Spreading the laundry over a nearby bush, she turned to the next item in the pile. How come it never grew any smaller?

Flexing the ache from her fingers, she plucked up a cerulean blue heap of dripping cotton. Her African-sky dress. A lurch of remembrance. Tannie Johanne straightening the collar, smoothing the folds of the skirt. With a sudden ferocity, Maria rolled the dress into a tight coil. Water cascaded through her protesting fingers, splattering the dust where she knelt. A faint scent of heated earth doused in cooling water. Maria breathed it in. Perhaps she could squeeze enough liquid from the washed dress that she'd be able to wear it later. As a tiny, private celebration of her birthday.

Tannie Susanna must not know it was her birthday. She'd sent her out on errands almost since daybreak.

"…fetch the eggs from Tannie Katerina's chickens. Then, young Martinus needs help with his spelling exercises as he's falling quite far behind the others, and a man must be able to read and write if he's to make anything of the new opportunities once we're settled. And then, there's washing I haven't had time to attend to. Oom Erasmus has been wearing the same shirt for three days." A wrinkle of the nose. "I will have to leave you to carry on by yourself. Something important has come to my attention and I must dedicate some time to dealing with it."

She'd passed a basket of soiled clothes from the rear of the wagon. Maria stifled her groans, anticipating the ache between the shoulder blades as she carried water from the river to heat over a smouldering fire she would need to cajole into flame; the wrinkled skin of her fingers as she scrubbed at the dirt and stains of camp life; the smell of the soap making her sneeze and her eyes water.

"I added a few of your things to the pile. Like your dress. You might as well do that while you're washing the other items."

Maria, registering slight surprise that Tannie Susanna should go through her belongings and sort her clothing on her behalf, had lugged the basket to a sunny spot beyond the encircled wagons, to return to it after collecting Tannie Katerina's eggs and locating the errant spelling master.

She'd hoped to bump into Christiaan as she strolled through the camp, but only the women bustled about, their children playing at their feet. Oom Erasmus, George and Salomon had saddled their horses and ridden off straight after their breakfast coffee and rusks. It seemed they weren't the only ones. Maybe Christiaan was right; others travelled the area seeking community, and the men had gone to meet them.

A boy of about ten hurtled towards her from behind a wagon. Martinus. She'd braced for impact, knowing his preferred greeting was to barge into her and wrap his arms around her legs, fixing her in place.

"Good morning, Tannie Maria." Brown eyes blinked up at her. "Ma says I have to do extra schoolwork with you today. But I don't want to. Can we go looking for birds, instead?"

"We'll see. I'm on my way to Tannie Katerina. She has eggs for Tannie Susanna. Do you want to join me?"

"Yes, please." Martinus nodded, untangling himself from her skirts. He placed a plump, sticky hand in her hers. "I'll take you there. I know where her wagon is."

"That's very kind of you. We'll take the eggs to Tannie Susanna, then do some of that work your ma spoke about." She smiled at the sag of the boy's shoulders, the sigh of resigned acceptance. "And if you get all your spellings right, we could learn how to write the names of the birds we see when we're done."

Martinus danced a jig at her side. "Oh, yes. There's a hoopoo nesting by the edge of the river. How do you spell that, Tannie Maria?"

He'd stood with solemn patience while Tannie Katrina packaged Tannie Susanna's eggs; skipped alongside as they returned to the Smit family wagon, chattering like one of the small birds he was so fond of. Although curious about Tannie Susanna's sudden need for eggs, Maria was prevented from asking anything by the eagerness of her young pupil to start with his lessons.

An hour and a half later, a page of loopy handwriting folded into his pocket, Martinus had scurried off in search of lunch. Leaving Maria to tackle the forgotten laundry.

She untangled the twisted blue of her dress and stretched it over a boulder warmed by the sun. It should dry quicker and so be wearable by the end of the day.

Maria slipped the final button into place. With no mirror, she couldn't be sure if the collar was straight, but she smoothed its lace against her collarbones. Mimmicking Tannie Johanne's fussing farewell. Would she be thinking of Maria today, praying the special birthday blessing, even though the recipient didn't occupy her seat at the table, didn't curl on a chair in the shade of the garden? Could such a blessing reach her, if uttered in her absence? The fog rolled thick and dark over the memories of birthdays past and rituals performed. No one here knew what day it was.

Except Christiaan. And he had forgotten. Or never intended seeking her out. Maria shoved the disappointment away with a sharp tug of her dangling plait. Why should she have expected him?

She reached for her bonnet from a stool. In the dim light of the tent, pitched alongside the wagon, she fumbled with the strings. She would settle beside the campfire and hope the dance of its flames would banish the fog with their warmth.

"Maria! Maria, where are you, child?" Tannie Susanna's piercing call shattered the quiet loneliness of the tent. Maria, startled by the unexpected intrusion into her few moments of solitude, choked on a breath caught in her throat.

"I'm here…" Coughing, she gulped for air.

"Where's here? Goodness, is that you coughing? Maria, are you alright?" The shrill call for her presence replaced with a note of concern. "Oh, you're in the tent. I'm coming in."

The distant hum of evening conversation increased in volume as the heavy canvas entrance flap swished open. A cool draught accompanied the voices. Tannie Susanna strode to Maria's side.

"That's it, deep breaths." She patted Maria's back.

Maria straightened, the coughing fit easing. "You were looking for me, Tannie Susanna?"

"Yes, yes, I need your help with something. But let me bring you a cup of water first. You stay here and recover yourself. Perhaps wipe your face with that face cloth there." She peered at Maria in the light from the open flap. "You look lovely, dear. Just wipe your face."

She bustled away, flicking the flap into place as she left. Mystified as to why Tannie Susanna wanted her to clean her face before performing whatever chore she had in mind for her, Maria plucked the cloth from the peg. She pressed it to her skin, its cool dampness calming the sting in her eyes from her choking.

Tannie Susanna returned with a swish and a bustle. "Here you are, drink this." She passed her a tin cup. Maria sipped the lukewarm water. The rawness of her throat eased. "Good, that's better. Now, leave that here and follow me."

Leaving the cup on the low stool, Maria hurried after Tannie Susanna's disappearing figure. "Aren't we finished with our work for the day, Tannie?" She tried to keep the complaint from her voice. No one else may know or care, but she would like to enjoy a free evening on her birthday.

Tannie Susanna waited beside an acacia tree. She waved her arms as though issuing instructions to someone, but Maria couldn't see anyone. She quickened her stride, curiosity beating annoyance.

"She's here!" Tannie Susanna flung an arm over Maria's shoulder, manoeuvring her past the tree and into the clearing beyond. "Happy birthday, Maria."

Tannie Susanna nudged Maria forward until she stood in the centre of a cheering, clapping circle of smiling faces lit by the flames of a blazing campfire. Oom Erasmus, less stern than usual. George, grinning and nodding. Salomon, hands in pockets but laughter in his eyes. A little girl clutching a bundle, shy behind the skirts of her mother. Debora.

In the shadows, an older lady, a shawl wrapped around her. Tannie Margarite. Maria hadn't seen her since the day she'd helped her on the mountain path.

Maria flicked her gaze from face to face. Searching. Hoping.

Foolish girl. He wasn't here. She swallowed.

"Tannie Johanne told us the date of your birthday before we left." Tannie Susanna held out a wrapped parcel. "We promised her we would celebrate, make your day special. I hope you enjoyed the surprise?" Anxious eyes searched Maria's face.

They'd gone to so much trouble. These were her family, her friends. Tannie Susanna must read gratitude and happiness and love on her face. Not the dismay of an unfulfilled promise made by an impolite stranger.

"It's wonderful…"

The snapping of twigs as footsteps approached. The quick breathing of someone in a hurry. The circle parting to allow another to enter.

"Sorry I'm late. Happy birthday, Maria." Christiaan. "I told you I'd see you today."

CHAPTER NINE

Klein Karoo, South Africa. October 1836

After the warm stillness of the previous night, the morning dawned damp and misty. Maria, clutching her shawl against the chill, strolled through the camp, enjoying a few moments alone before Tannie Susanna recalled her to her chores. Gusts of spring wind gathered the last of winter's fallen leaves into dancing pirouettes, swirling and twisting in the eddies of air.

Recollections of her birthday party filled her mind, snapshots of an evening of laughter and firelight and companionship. Tannie Susanna leading her to the centre of the circle of well-wishers; Debora rushing forward with a bunch of drooping flowers and a strip of knitted yarn tied into a bow. "For your hair, Tannie Maria."

Oom Erasmus praying a word of blessing over both her and the food, and Tannie Margarite kissing her cheek and saying how much like her mother she looked in the sky blue dress.

And Christiaan, hovering on the outskirts of the celebration, chatting to George or teasing Saloman about his shooting ability. The certainty of his eyes on her, watching her as she danced with Debora or laughed with Tannie Margarite.

He'd left before the singing started, bowing a farewell from the shadows of the firelight. Taking some of the night's sparkle with him.

Two or three songs later, and the party drew to a close. Someone stamped the fire out. Maria curled into her bed, hugging the parcel from Tannie Johanne to her for opening in the morning.

The present rustled in her pocket as she walked. Finding a sheltered spot out of the wind, she retrieved the parcel, her breath catching at the sight of familiar spidery handwriting.

Dearest Maria. With birthday blessings. Tannie Johanne.

She tugged at the string holding the paper in place. Tears prickled as Maria unfolded a thick, cream-coloured linen. Delicate embroidered flowers in pink, blue and orange, entwined with dark green ivy stems and leaves, patterned the fabric's edge. Lines of Scripture looped and curled in its centre.

For I know the plans I have for you, says the Lord, plans for welfare and not for evil, to give you a future and a hope.

And a crooked letter P.

Maria laughed out loud, the sudden noise sending a weaver bird hurrying from its nest in twittering alarm.

"What has you so amused?" Christiaan. Maria's heart echoed the fleeing chirrups of the bird. She stuffed Tannie Johanne's gift into the apron pocket with one hand, wiping any evidence of tears from her eyes with the other.

"Do you always creep up on people?" Maria hopped down from the rock where she perched. "Or is it only me?"

"I really didn't mean to. I just seem to find you when you're lost in a different place. Who was your present from?"

Maria held a protective hand over her pocket. "My aunt. From home."

"Tannie Johanne. The one who arranged our party all the way from Graaff-Reinet."

"Yes, I suppose she did." Maria hadn't thought of it that way, but supposed it was true. If Tannie Johanne hadn't urged the Smit family to plan something, her birthday would have gone unnoticed.

Or would it? Christiaan shuffled beside her, avoiding her look as she tried to catch his eye.

"What?" A giggle at his evident discomfort. "Did you follow me here, Christiaan?"

"Well, I — " In one hurried movement, Christiaan pulled something from his jacket pocket and pushed it into Maria's hands. "I wanted to give this to you yesterday, but there wasn't a chance. I couldn't get you alone for a minute. So, yes, perhaps I did notice you leave your wagon earlier, and perhaps I did happen to find myself on the same path as you and…Oh, I'm such a fool, aren't I?"

Maria's grin spread from her face to her shaking shoulders and aching sides.

Christiaan joined in the laughter. They collapsed onto Maria's rock. "Go on, open it. I made it especially for you."

"You made it?" Maria fumbled with the knot of coarse twine. She unwrapped the brown paper, revealing a small wooden cross looped onto a length of thin leather. "A necklace? You made me a necklace?"

She stared at the gift, a lump forming in her throat as she pictured Christiaan hunched over his handiwork, whittling a piece of wood with the hunting knife always tucked into his belt.

"Do you like it?" An eagerness to please tinged with a hint of doubt. "Perhaps it's not the sort of thing you wear. And I'm not really very good at carving yet. The others in the commando are teaching me a few techniques, helping me improve. I can make another one…"

Maria flung her arms around his neck, silencing the flow of words. "I love it. Thank you. You're so clever. You're the best big brother I could ever want."

Brother? Was that what they were? Brother and sister? Of course, what else would they be?

Christiaan extricated himself from her hug, prising her hands apart. For a brief second, his searching Tannie Johanne eyes fastened on hers. With a whoosh of escaping breath, her heart leapt under his scrutiny. He blinked, hiding unspoken questions, retreating to the safety of friendship.

"Let me put it on for you." He plucked the necklace from Maria's lap. She swivelled around, her back to him, grateful for the moment to calm the surprising flutteriness in her stomach. His fingers tickled her neck as he shifted her plait to one side, then knotted the leather string. "There. Now, let's see."

His hands on her shoulders, he turned her to face him. She tugged on the necklace, rubbing the smooth edges of the carved wood between her thumb and forefinger.

"So? How does it look?" She released the necklace, allowing it to dangle free, conscious of the weight of his hands still on her shoulders.

"It looks exactly how I imagined it would…" Christiaan lifted his hands and jumped from the boulder. Shoving his fists into his pockets, he took a couple of steps away, not looking at Maria. "Maria, we're leaving."

"Leaving?" The fog floated across the sunshine of the gift hanging from her neck. "When? Why? Where are you going?"

"The commando is needed on other frontiers. Some of the tribal leaders don't want us on their lands. So we're told." He kicked at a stone. "We leave today. This morning."

The dripping of water from the trees loud. A bird calling to its mate. A rushing in Maria's head. Quickened breathing. She bent double, gasping for air like a fish deprived of water.

"Steady. Slow breaths." His face looming close. "I'm sorry. I didn't realise it would be such a shock. I should have warned you."

Maria's vision cleared. "I'm fine. Haven't eaten yet." She shoved Christiaan away, gritting her teeth against a wave of dizziness as she forced herself upright. "If you're leaving now, you'd best get going then. You don't want to be late for Commandant Prinsloo."

She despised the sneer in her voice, the curl of her lips, but was powerless to prevent them. A storm flashed and thundered inside. Her only companion on this wretched journey, leaving. Abandoning her.

"Maria, I…"

"Go." The thunder cracked and exploded, threatening to spill over in a torrent of bitter, angry tears. She wouldn't let him see. Wouldn't let him know what his absence meant. "And take your stupid gift with you…"

She yanked at the cross, desperate for the leather to snap and break so she could hurl it at his feet. Discard it to the ground. An echo of herself.

Christiaan leapt forward, hands curling over hers. "No. Don't do that." A calloused thumb stroked her wrist. "Please keep it. I'll be back, I promise. I'll find you."

The storm clouds parted. A chink of sunshine. Could she believe him?

"I promise, Maria."

CHAPTER TEN

Welkom, South Africa. October 1837

Maria dropped the barrel to the ground with a thump. A prickly pear rolled from the top of the pile, dislodged by her aggravation. What was the point of dwelling on that? Time moved on, things changed. Promises got broken.

As did Tannie Susanne's heart. Salomon — favoured youngest son, light of her life, joy of her days — couldn't survive the rigours of this transient, in-between life they all clung to. Maria retrieved the pear, her mind playing again the images of an unwanted July burial. Shivering in her only black dress; the ground hard and unyielding to the gravedigger's shovel; Oom Erasmus stumbling over the words of committal and the prayers of mourning for his son. Winter aloes, resplendent shards of burnt orange and crimson red soaring from spikey leaves. A grave marker fashioned from a broken, discarded packing crate.

And Tannie Susanne, retreating to the unreachable refuge of twenty-one years of memories and moments. Midway through a task, her attention wandered and her expression slackened, leaving Maria to step in and finish the lesson or complete the row. Half-eaten meals were scraped into the dogs' bowls. Conversation between husband and wife became monosyllabic instructions and responses.

Maria wedged the pear amongst the others and bent to take the weight of the barrel once more.

"Here, let me take that for you." George tethered his horse to a tree and strode over the grass towards her.

George. The unloved, living son. He roamed the plains with his friends, hunting on horseback or trekking on foot for hour after hour. Anything to distance himself from the morose silence Tannie Susanna maintained in his presence. For Maria, a twist of compassion always accompanied his appearance. He must miss his brother, too.

Maria blew a curl of hair from her eyes. "Thank you, George. Your ma wants it taken to the de Villiers' wagon. Said there's no space in ours." She relinquished her burden to George's care. "Although why we need more room, I'm not sure. We're not going anywhere, are we?"

George hefted the barrel. He gave her a sidelong glance, surprise in his raised eyebrows. "You mean you don't know? About Oom Piet's proposal?"

"Oom Piet?" She recognised the name, although couldn't place it. Not one of their party. She hurried to catch up with George, her skirts swishing through the long summer grass.

"Yes, Piet Retief and a group of his supporters. The ones who joined us earlier this year."

An image of a man in his mid-fifties, neat beard, very outspoken against the British if anyone asked his opinion, flitted into Maria's mind. "Oh, yes, I remember him. They appointed him leader for a while, didn't they? What about him?"

"Have you really not heard?" George stopped, put the barrel down, watched Maria through narrowed eyes.

"George, heard what? You're frightening me. What's happening?" Maria plucked at George's shirt, willing him to explain. The pears could wait.

George scrubbed a hand through his beard. "I can't believe Ma hasn't told you. Well, I suppose I can. Oom Piet has decided to leave the colony here and instead make for Natal. Over the mountains."

"And? What does that have to do with us? With me?" A wisp of fog. A year of being settled, of joining with the other Voortrekkers Christiaan had spoken of, had lulled Maria into a sense of blissful security she shouldn't have allowed herself to encourage. After all, they still lived out of a covered wagon in a makeshift canvas tent; no one built any permanent homes or planted more than a few vegetables alongside the river.

Snatches of overheard midnight conversations clicked into place.

"...we should consider it, Susanna. A smaller community, more opportunities..."

"...I don't want to, Erasmus...leave Salomon..."

"...new start...good for you...new responsibilities..."

Maria sucked in a sudden breath. "George, are we going with him? Into Natal?"

"Maria, I didn't mean to upset you. I truly thought you would know." George gripped her hand, rubbing it between his own. "It's all been decided. We outspan in a few days' time. As soon as Oom Gert settles a few matters with the rest of the leadership."

"That's why your ma has had me washing and sorting everything, isn't it? I thought it was a kind of spring cleaning. Maybe even that she was recovering from...from..."

"From my brother." George squeezed her hand before releasing it. "No, she isn't recovering from that. Don't tell anyone, but I'm considering not travelling with you. I might see about joining your friend's commando instead. It's not as though they'll notice if I'm not here."

"What friend? I think you and Tannie Margarite are my only friends here." And now you're leaving as well. Why should she have expected something different?

"I'm glad, Maria, that you consider me your friend. And I will be sorry to leave you." He shook his head. "No, there is another friend, I believe. That boy you hung about with last summer. What was his name?"

Maria's fingers strayed to the wooden cross hung at her neck. "Oh, Christiaan Venter? He rode with Andries Pretorious, didn't he?" Heat warmed her cheeks. "He's not a particular friend."

"No?" The raised eyebrows. "You could have fooled me."

"No, George. We were perhaps friends while he was here, but he's gone and that's an end to it." Maria hid the necklace in the folds of her shawl. "And you'll forget me, too."

CHAPTER ELEVEN

Kerkenberg, South Africa. January 1838

"We'll take that route there. Do you see the track?" Piet Retief shielded his eyes from the sun with a hand to his forehead, his hat pushed back.

"Yes, that looks a suitable option." Oom Gert, standing alongside, nodded.

Maria squinted to find the track they referred to. Tannie Susanna and the other women stood a respectful distance from the men, but within earshot of their discussion.

The plain spread out below them, a patchwork of meadows and fields intersected by a glistening ribbon of a flowing river. In the distance, the purple outline of more mountains ringed the valley. An occasional dwelling punctuated the landscape, with a curl of smoke rising into the air. Dark shapes dotted the brighter green of some fields. Cattle.

"Natal. A new home for a new republic." Oom Piet turned to his followers, his face animated and his grey eyes gleaming with pioneering fervour. "The Lord has brought us thus far, and will carry us forward into a place of green pastures and rest."

Rest. What was that? Thirteen wagons, laden with everything from food and clothing to fruit trees and farm tools, had plodded their way across the wilderness seeking this mythical attainment. According to George, Oom Piet had sent scouts ahead, declaring the land beyond the Drakensberg mountain range their God-promised destination.

He'd then embraced Maria a final time and ridden away in search of Andries Pretorius and his commando.

"That boy should have stayed with us. Been here to help with the wagon, drive the oxen, protect you womenfolk." A daily refrain from Oom Erasmus.

"We'll manage." Tannie Susanna, tight-lipped. "We did before, when Salomon…"

Tears. So many tears.

"We'll never get down there." Debora's mother, Tannie Isobel. Her whisper seemed to echo the fear of the others, several nodding or muttering in agreement. "The wagons won't make the descent without running out of control."

"Nonsense." Tannie Susanna's confident response. She may mourn and grieve and have little to say in the privacy of their wagon, but when confronted with the nervous fears of others, she rose to her place as leader. "Oom Piet and Gert will have a plan, of that I'm certain. And as Erasmus frequently sermonises, when the Lord is with us, who or what shall be against us? We are assured of His presence and provision even in the matter of our travel."

Tannie Susanna sounded so certain, so unwavering. Maria watched as the men gesticulated and pointed down the hillside, deep in discussion. Piet Retief, his tall frame towering over the huddle, swivelled his attention from one man to another as they voiced their ideas. Ideas too jumbled and inarticulate for Maria to hear.

She turned towards the camp. Whatever the decision, whatever the plan, one thing was certain; she would need to have everything ready for an imminent departure. Standing around listening to the niggle of her fears being aired by Tannie Isobel and her companions wouldn't prepare the wagon for its journey downhill.

Tree branches. That was the solution.

"We'll remove the rear wheels of the wagons and tie thick branches in their place." Oom Erasmus indicated the wagon, pink spots on his cheeks highlighting his enthusiasm for the project. His words spilled over themselves in a rush of excitement. "It's such a wonderful solution. The branches will protect the axles from damage — the rocks and stones in the pathway, you know — and also act as a sort of brake. It's very clever. All Piet's idea, of course. Really, he is a remarkable man. Gert did the right thing, choosing to join with his party and continue our journey with him."

"So you keep saying. Let's hope our destination proves to be worth the effort of getting there. If we do so in one piece." Tannie Susanna cocked her head sideways, seeming to eye the wagon with distrust. "Maria, we must encourage the women to ensure they pack and secure all their belongings, while the men gather sufficient branches or whatever they need to implement their plan."

For the next week, the camp at Kerkenberg resembled a lumberjack's yard. The constant sound of axe against tree accompanied the deep-voiced instructions of the men, the shrill panic of the women. Oxen dragged the felled branches into position, their drivers urging and cajoling them with clicks of the tongue and flicks of their whips. Children dodged in and out, their games resulting in shouts and clips to the ear as they got in everyone's way.

Maria shared her time between following Tannie Susanna from wagon to wagon, assisting with the safe storage of baskets and boxes, and occupying the children with games and activities designed to keep them from trouble. A growing excitement bubbled up, bursting out in sudden laughter or spilling over in song.

"You seem happy, child. All this activity is good for your heart, I think." Tannie Margarite handed Maria a bundle of cloth. "Wrap the clock in this. It should be safe."

"Did you bring it from your farm?" Maria lay the clock on the square of fabric. "The carving on the face is beautiful."

"It is, isn't it? It was a gift." A pause. "Maria, leave that for a moment. Come and sit with me. I want to talk, enjoy the peace of the afternoon instead of burying ourselves in the exhaustion of preparations."

"But Tannie Susanna…"

"Susanna Smit can wait. She's always in a bustle over something." Tannie Margarite patted the grass beside her stool. "This is more important."

Maria folded the fabric over the clock, then shuffled next to Tannie Margarite. "What's important?"

"Do you remember I told you I knew your mother once, a long time ago?"

Maria nodded, her mouth dry and her pulse flickering.

"I've been thinking, since that day, how to explain everything to you. How I knew her, and the rest of your family." She rested an age-spotted hand on Maria's shoulder. "I made such a mess of it before, blurting it out without thinking first. I could see that shocked — and hurt — you. But I've prayed, asked the Lord to give me another opportunity to explain properly. I said Johanne and I were friends, didn't I? In truth, we're more than friends. We're related."

"Related? Why would she not have mentioned you then? She's never mentioned any family." Maria jerked free from Tannie Margarite's touch. "Sorry, that was rude. I…"

"Don't apologise. I'd be rude too, if I suddenly discovered I had family I didn't know about. Because I am your family, Maria. Distant, but family nonetheless."

"How…?" Maria's insides tumbled and rolled. Like she imagined the wagons would do when they descended the narrow track into Natal.

"There I go again. Giving you snippets of information without the details. Let me start at the beginning." Tannie Margarite settled on her seat, her eyes half closed in remembrance. "My father was the brother of your Oupa and Tannie Johanne's mother — of your great-grandmother. She was my aunt, and your Oupa and Johanne were, are, my cousins. We grew up on neighbouring farms, in and out of each other's homes, sharing meals. And beds, more often than not."

A chuckle.

Maria, head spinning, traced a few lines in the dusty soil of the patch of ground where they sat. "So that makes you my great-aunt? Am I right?"

"That's it! And you're the great-niece I've always hoped to meet. Imagine how surprised I was when you came to my aid on that mountain path. It was as if the years rolled back and it was your mother, my niece, coming to my rescue. You really do look like her, you know."

Maria ducked away from Tannie Margarite's scrutiny. She wasn't yet ready to hear those comparisons. "But the clock? What does that have to do with anything?"

"Oh, yes, the clock. It was made by your Oupa. That beautiful carving? He did all that himself. Sat for hour after hour in the evenings, whittling at the wood with his knife by only the light of the fire in their kitchen. He must have been only about twenty. I used to watch him when I visited, fascinated at the shapes he could create in a piece of wood." She stretched, flicked the folded fabric open to reveal the clockface again. "You see that bit there? Where the curve isn't quite even?"

Maria peered at the intricate pattern. She hadn't noticed the squared-off curl earlier.

"I did that! I so wanted to carve and practised with bits of wood lying around before plucking up the courage to ask Hendrik — your Oupa — to allow me to work on his clock." She huffed out her cheeks. "To his credit, he didn't shout when my finger slipped and I made that mistake. Only wanted to check that I hadn't cut myself. Which I had, of course. You can still see the scar all these years later. Look."

She held out a wrinkled finger. Slashed across its tip, a deeper line distinguishable from the folds of age.

"When they left for Graaff-Reinet, he gave me the clock. Said it was too bulky to carry. It's been on my mantelpiece ever since." She struggled from her stool, stiff joints making her wince as she straightened, then bent to pull the clock from its protective covering. "He was right about it being bulky. But I'm sure you'll manage with it."

Tannie Margarite eased herself back into her seat, the clock cradled in her lap.

"I brought it in the hope we would meet, as Johanne believed we would. It was only on loan to me, really. It needs to be reunited with its rightful owner." She reached for Maria's hand, pressing it onto the clock. "It belongs to you, Maria. You shall take it with you and set it on your own mantelpiece one day."

"No!" Maria snatched her hand from under Tannie Margarite's, scrabbling to her feet. She clutched her arms around her waist, desperate to still the shivers trembling through her. Tannie Johanne only spoke once or twice about the old days, but each time Maria became too upset for her to continue her reminiscences. And now here was this white-haired old woman, someone she'd met by chance and whose gentle friendship she'd enjoyed for the last year, throwing her words like pebbles into a lake, not caring who she splashed or where the ripples spread.

A white-haired old woman who turned out to be family.

CHAPTER TWELVE

Kerkenberg, South Africa. January 1838

Family. A moan escaped from Maria before her clamped lips could prevent it.

Tannie Margarite was at her side, the clock discarded in the grass. Fingers fluttered against her back, tickled her bare arms. Maria tried to pull away, but a bony grip held her in place. The confusion; the realised longing for others beside herself and Tannie Johanne in the world, the fear it would be stripped from her; all too much. With a shuddering breath. Maria burst into tears. Hot, ugly tears streamed unchecked down her face. Her nose dripped the secretions of misery. The fog shifted and formed black clouds of a despair Maria could no longer keep at bay.

"Ssh, child, ssh."

"But if you — give the clock — it means — you're not — coming — as well…" The storm reinvigorated at another thought. "I find you — and then — and then…"

"You fear you will lose me, and all connection to the family you long for, isn't that right?"

A gulp and sniff Maria's reply.

"The clock holds more than the time in its hands. Come, let me show you." Tannie Margarite steered Maria to the stool. She pulled over an upturned crate and sat on it, her knees touching Maria's. Retrieving the clock, she placed it in Maria's lap, its face resting in the folds of her skirt. "Do you see that little door there? My fingers are too clumsy now to open it. You do it."

Maria examined the door, her vision blurring as she imagined a grandfather she'd never met bent over a hunk of wood, forming and shaping it into the timepiece she held. Curiosity wormed through misgivings. Using her fingernail to slide along the slenderest of gaps, she prised open the tiny door. Silver cogs gleamed in the light.

"It's only the inner workings of the clock, Tannie Margarite. There's nothing else inside." Sympathy for the old woman's loss of memory, or whatever it was, vied with disappointment.

"Oh, but you're not looking carefully enough. There. That brown pouch. Take it out."

Hidden in the shadows of the casing, Maria hadn't noticed the slim leather wallet. She reached inside the clock, wiggling the pouch free. A strip of faded lace held it closed.

"Open it." Tannie Margarite sounded as excited as a child at Christmas. What on earth was in the wallet?

Her excitement was contagious. With trembling fingers, and all lonely sorrow banished, for the moment at least, Maria picked at the knotted lace. It came free with a determined tug. The pouch, folded in two like the cover of a book, flopped open as the tension holding it in place released.

Maria stared at yellowed sheets of paper, tiny letters criss-crossing the pages. A curl of blond hair rested on top.

"They were your mother's things. She hid them in there when they left. Explained she wanted them to be like buried treasure for any children she might have some day." Tannie Margarite tapped a finger on the pile. "It was her way of stopping time, perhaps."

"But — " Maria fought to arrange her scurrying thoughts into some sort of order. "You said she was only fifteen when you last saw her. A year younger than me. She wouldn't be thinking about children at that age. I'm certainly not."

Her hand strayed to the wooden cross around her neck, toyed with it for a moment. She wasn't thinking of marriage, let alone children. Was she?

"You have to remember, things were different then. Your oupa and ouma had already decided your mother would marry

Sarel. Your father. It's partly why they moved from the farm and went to Graaff-Reinet. To be nearer to his family." Tannie Margarite breathed out a sigh. "Your mother's heart was always with her grandparents. She loved them dearly, spent almost all of every day with them when she was younger. The keepsakes offered a connection between them, as well as ensuring her children discovered their roots. That's a lock of her hair. The same colour as yours."

Maria stroked the circle of hair, not daring to pick it up in case the wind caught it and snatched it away. A vague memory stirred. The tickle of hair the colour of sunshine against her cheek. A tinkle of laughter like a breeze through trees. The scent of flowers. Ma.

"You're right, I won't make the journey into Natal with you, Maria." The memory faded at Tannie Margarite's words. Maria's throat closed over another cry. "A few of us are returning to the colony at Welkom. We came this far to see the country you'll call home, but know we can't make the journey beyond here. But don't be afraid, Maria. you'll continue and you'll carry this piece of me, of your great-grandparents, of Tannie Johanne. Most importantly, of your mother. You've heard that Scripture in the book of Hebrews, about the cloud of witnesses watching and encouraging you onwards?"

Maria chewed on her lip, screwing her eyes up against a further spill of tears. "Yes, I think so."

"That's us. Your family, cheering you on as you step into the fullness of your new life. Whenever you wind this clock, listen to its ticking, allow it to remind you of this one truth; you belong, dear one, and you are never alone."

Maria scrambled alongside the creaking wagon as it shunted downhill, the oxen grunting and blowing against its weight. The tree branch brakes were working; four wagons had navigated the pass down the mountain without incident. Oom Erasmus trotted up and down on his horse, looking as proud of himself as if the innovation were his own. Oom Gert already waited at the bottom, his being one of the first wagons to attempt the treacherous descent. Piet Retief brought up the rear, stating in a loud voice his intention to ensure the safety of the whole party.

Maria hopped from grassy tussock to grassy tussock with her skirts bunched in her left hand to prevent them from being torn. In her other, she wielded a stick rescued from the piles of unused branches from camp. With it, she prodded the ground ahead, checking for snakes or any covered holes in which she could fall and twist an ankle. Her heart felt as light as her tread, and her voice rose in a series of songs and choruses. It was the strangest thing, but at each replay of the conversation with Tannie Marguerite, when she recalled the part about belonging, rather than the fog creeping in to smother her, the sun seemed instead to shine brighter.

A red-chested rock jumper bird accompanied Maria down the slope. At a pause in its playful chirping, Maria stopped to watch it hunting the dirt for insects.

"I wish I could stop and eat something, Mr Bird. I'm starving." The hurried breakfast of slurped coffee and dunked rusks at dawn was hours ago. Her stomach grumbled.

"We'll stop as soon as we're over this rough bit." Tannie Susanna waited in the shade of a tree. Her face gleamed with perspiration. "It's too hot to continue much further, anyway. We'll rest until the day is cooler and let the drivers keep going with the wagons without us."

"Is that a good idea? What if we're separated or get lost?" Maria didn't fancy a night perched on the edge of a mountain.

"I don't think that's likely. Look, we can easily follow where the track goes. Gert's team cleared much of the vegetation as they journeyed."

Maria narrowed her eyes against the midday glare. The track cut a clear swathe through the bushes and summer grasses of the lower slopes. Reassured, she squatted next to Tannie Susanna.

"Let's stop here then. It's quite sheltered from the sun. And I can call for Immanuel to jog to us with some food and water. I'm sure he wouldn't mind."

Immanuel, the youngest of their servants, had a soft spot for Maria and would do whatever she asked.

"Poor Immanuel, we can't have him running up here when he's so far ahead of us. No, we won't do that. I carried a small cannister of water and some biltong with me. So we'll have a brief rest now and refresh ourselves enough to continue, in the hope our absence is noted and they pause to wait for us." Tannie Susanna delved into the linen bag at her feet. "Ah ha, and I have apricots for us. Here you are."

"Thank you." Maria sucked on the soft flesh of the apricot. Juice dribbled down her chin and onto her bonnet strings. She giggled. "This reminds me of picnics with Tannie Johanne when I was little. She used to take me to the river to play and always packed apricots as a treat."

The rock jumper flitted in amongst the leaves of the tree. An orange butterfly no bigger than a flower petal flicked past.

"You've seemed happier these past few days, Maria. We were becoming concerned." Tannie Susanna plucked at a blade of grass. "I say we. George spoke to me before he left. Told me to keep an eye on you. It's the last conversation we had…"

Maria paused mid-bite. "George spoke to you? He promised he wouldn't." A bitter tang tinged the sweetness of the fruit.

"Oh, don't be upset with him. He cares for you like a little sister. I sometimes wish I'd had more children. He would have been good with them, especially if they were girls. Unlike Salomon, who, truth be told, wanted my attention all to himself." Maria almost choked on her mouthful of fruit at this unexpected confession. Tannie Susanna must be suffering from the heat more than she realised. "I hear what you all say, that Salomon was the only child I loved. And I suppose you're correct, in a way. But I did — do — love George. I just don't understand him. Never have. His temperament is so different to my own, you see."

A vision of George, head thrown back in riotous laughter as he galloped on an unsaddled horse, his hands clinging to the animal's mane. Tannie Susanna was right, he was so unlike his careful mother. Maria swallowed her amusement.

"But I'm not talking about George. Only to say he wanted to make me aware of how hard this all is for you. Leaving Tannie Johanne to travel with us, not really able to make friends with the other girls your age because you're seen as the pastor's child, the leader's special project." She patted Maria's knee, easing the sting of her words. "I don't mean that harshly. It's just he knows what that's like, has endured others' jokes and unfair comments all his life. I'm glad he went with Andries Pretorius. He won't have history with those men. He can be simply George, from Graaff-Reinet."

Maria wiped her sticky hands on a rag pulled from her pocket. Words half-formed then evaporated before reaching her lips. What could she say in response to Tannie Susanna's unusual frankness?

"I expected you would find leaving Tannie Margarite a wrench. You've grown closer to her recently than you seem to have been all year. Oh, I know you were friends already, but this seemed different. More intense." Tannie Susanna peered from under the brim of her bonnet, a frown wrinkling her forehead. "But here you are, singing like a lark."

Maria reached for the water. "Yes, I also thought it would be too hard to bear. Saying farewell to Tannie Johanne was the worst feeling. Well, except one other…" She sipped at the water to cool the sudden burn in her throat. "But something she said clicked everything into place like…like…"

"A row of stitches in Debora's knitting?"

Maria spluttered on the water. "Yes, yes, exactly like that." She handed the drink to Tannie Susanna, their fingers brushing in an easy and unexpected companionship. Maybe Tannie Margarite was right and the next chapter of her life would prove less lonely than the first. And maybe in her future there was a mantelpiece for her clock — her family clock — and a husband to hear the tick of her heart.

The leather string of a hand-carved necklace rubbed against her throat.

CHAPTER THIRTEEN

Sooilaer, Natal, South Africa. January 1838

Lightning slashed the sky, a jagged line of brilliant white in the cloudless blue of the summer sky. Maria straightened from the furrow she dug in the sun-baked soil.

"One...two...three..." She counted the seconds between the flash and the first distant rumble of approaching thunder. Still far off. She should manage to finish her task before the rain came.

"Storm coming. We'd better hurry." Tannie Susanna called over from the patch of ground she worked. "I want to plant these beans before we're forced to abandon work for the day. I smell the rain already."

Maria inhaled. The sweet scent of thirsty earth receiving droplets of heaven-sent water lingered. She wiped her forehead with the edge of her apron.

"It will be a relief when the storm does break. I can hardly breath in this heat." Tannie Susanna stretched, rubbing the small of her back with clenched fists. "And at least we'll have a rest from all this digging and planting. I'm not sure Gert realised it would be quite this difficult."

Perhaps he expected more men to remain behind, assist with the hard labour. Maria didn't speak the thought out loud. There was enough bitterness and division in the group, she wouldn't add her feelings into the mix. She grabbed her hoe and returned to her task. These seeds wouldn't plant themselves.

"I believe Piet Retief and his men were successful in their meeting with that native leader." Tannie Isobel grunted as she tugged at a clump of grass. "No, Debora, we must clear the area first, then plant your cabbages."

"Now where did you hear that, Isobel?" Tannie Susanna's disapproval of the woman's gossip sharpened her tone of voice. Maria held her breath. She longed for news of the negotiations Oom Piet was supposed to be having with the tribal king, but each time she tried to ask a question, Tannie Susanna shushed her with remonstrations that this was no business for the women.

Maria disagreed.

Since arriving in Natal, disagreements between Oom Gert and Piet Retief escalated from mild doubts spoken in light-hearted friendship to shouted arguments and the eventual parting of company. Piet Retief, accompanied by his son Pieter Cornelis, rode away with a delegation of one hundred men, declaring they would negotiate settlement rights with the Zulu leader, Dingaan. Oom Gert, his jaw clenched and expression determined, declined to travel with the party and instead led the remaining group of non-fighting men, women, and children to their present encampment beside the river.

Arranging the wagons in a horseshoe alongside the river, Oom Gert ordered the drivers and servants to add further defences, building an earth rampart around and between the wagons. His conviction of an impending attack infected the whole camp, and a jittery tension pervaded the atmosphere. Many spoke of leaving Natal and returning to the colony in Welkom. Some did exactly that.

"We can't afford to be alone here for so long." Last night's overheard conversation between Oom Gert and Oom Erasmus troubled Maria as she prepared the soil for planting. A faint dizziness was from more than the intensity of the day's heat. "If Retief's plan fails, we are vulnerable to a counter attack."

Oom Erasmus' stool creaked as he shifted his position. "Gert, you have to be careful. Don't be too alarmist. Your speaking of these things is frightening the people. We must encourage vigilance, of course, and do all we can to protect ourselves. But we have to remember this is the land the Lord has brought us to. We should uplift the people with His promises, not dash their hopes with our doomsaying."

"Prayers are all well and good, Erasmus." Oom Gert must be pacing back and forth, his voice alternating between muffled and clear as Maria strained to catch his replies. "But we also need wisdom. Retief should never have gone to Dingaan himself; he should have sent emissaries instead. He is needed alive as leader, not dead."

Maria clamped a hand over her mouth to prevent her from crying out and revealing her presence. They wouldn't respond well to her eavesdropping. Dead? Why did Oom Gert speak of Piet Retief as dead?

"You exaggerate, Gert. Your fears are getting the better of you." Oom Erasmus spoke with a confidence Maria hoped he meant. "Retief is an excellent judge of character. And well able to look after himself if the discussions become unpleasant. It's been a little over a week since he left. Give him time. He'll return with his treaty signed and the land will be ours That's why we came here, don't forget. For a place of our own, where we govern as we see fit. And as the Lord leads."

Maybe Tannie Isobel had heard more of Piet Retief's expedition, despite what Tannie Susanna said. Although from where, Maria couldn't guess. No outsider arrived at the camp without everyone knowing of it.

She sidled over in the hopes she could persuade further conversation out of Tannie Susanna's hearing.

"That looks hard work, Debora. Shall I help you?"

The child looked up, her face streaked with dirt and sweat. "We have to make space for the cabbages. That's what Ma says. And these weeds are in the way." She shuffled over, making space for Maria.

"How about I help you? If we do it together, that might be better . What do you think?"

"I don't know, Tannie Maria." Doubt crinkled the girl's nose.

"Let's try. Ready? Pull!" With a heave and a grunt from Debora, the earth released its grip on the handful of weeds. Soil showered down over them both, covering them in sand and debris. "Goodness, Debora, you really are very strong. You didn't need my help at all."

"Look, Ma. I got it out. And Tannie Maria didn't do anything."

"What a clever girl you are, Debora." Tannie Isobel winked at Maria, her eyes dancing with laughter. "But you are also now a very dirty girl. We should pack away our things and hurry to camp to clean up before the storm hits."

"Oh, but what about the cabbages?"

A fat raindrop plopped to the ground. "We'll let the rain soften everything a bit and finish the job tomorrow." She reached for Debora's hand. "Come on, let's get back before we're soaked. Tannie Susanna, I'm going to help Tannie Isobel with Debora. Is that alright?"

Tannie Susanna waved a hand in dismissal. "I'll be right behind you. One more beanstalk. Oh…"

A crack of thunder. The clouds burst open, deluging the women with torrents of rain.

"Quick, we'll make a run for it." Maria hoisted Debora into her arms and sloshed through the puddles to camp.

"You said you'd heard that Piet Retief's party had success?" Maria cradled the steaming mug of coffee in her hands. Water dripped from the canvas opening of the tent. Rivulets of muddy water criss-crossed the entrance, held at bay by another roll of canvas retrieved from the wagon. Debora lay curled on her cot in a thick blanket, her eyes closed and her breathing deep with sleep.

"I don't think Susanna would like you asking. Do you?" Tannie Isobel stroked a strand of hair from her daughter's face.

"She won't know, Tannie Isobel. I won't tell her. I just want to know what's happening, that's all. I'm not a child anymore." Maria raised her chin, daring Tannie Isobel to contradict her.

Tannie Isobel laughed. "No, Maria, you're not a child. You're only a few years younger than me, aren't you?" She took a sip of coffee. "Yes, I did hear a recent report. From one of the servants. He'd been to collect supplies for me. Those cabbages? He arrived early this morning. According to the locals he met, Dingaan asked Oom Piet to retrieve some cattle stolen by a rival tribe. Of course, that would be an easy task, with their weapons and so on."

"And? What happened next?"

"He didn't know. Only that everyone was pleased with the outcome and that Dingaan had ordered all his tribesmen to attend a celebration in the next day or so." Tannie Isobel shrugged. "So I suppose that means we'll settle in something more permanent than a wagon and a tent. With a roof that doesn't leak, I hope."

CHAPTER FOURTEEN

Sooilaer, South Africa. 7 February 1838

An eerie quietness hung over the camp. Even the birds were silent.

Maria couldn't decide if it was the stillness following days of storms or something more ominous. Increased activity around Oom Gert's wagon since the previous afternoon had started a whispering rumour about trouble for Piet Retief's party, but Tannie Susanna had frowned away questions. And Maria wasn't able to manufacture a visit to Tannie Isobel in search of more information.

Sighing, she pulled the next item of mending from the basket at her side. Tannie Susanna's offer to be the community seamstress had received several grateful responses, all of which she passed to Maria for her attention. The pile of torn clothes, missing buttons, and loosened collars seemed to increase daily, with Maria hunched on her stool for hour after dreary hour, while the wind and rain buffeted the tent.

At least today the sun shone. A circle of vultures whirled on the thermals high in the clearest of blue skies. The river bordering the camp raced past in a foaming, tumbling torrent of floodwater. An overriding smell of mud and damp fabric added to Maria's unease.

"It will take some time for the soil to dry out." Tannie Susanna squelched through a slick of mud at the entrance to the tent. "We shan't be doing any planting for another couple of days, I shouldn't think. Take yourself outside and you can work on that sewing. Finish it before we return to the fields."

"I'm not sure I'll ever be finished. I have blisters on my fingers and my thumb is rubbed raw from shoving the needle through those woollen overcoats of Oom Dirk's." Maria knew she sounded whiney and out of sorts, but couldn't stop herself. Her head throbbed, her neck a crunchy mass of knots. This sort of sewing was nothing like the gentle embroidery she enjoyed with Tannie Johanne.

"You'll be alright after you've had some fresh air. It's being cooped up in here, that's the problem." Tannie Susanna shooed her through the tent flap. "And speaking of coops, I need to assist Elisabeth with her chickens. A few of them got out in the storm and she needs me to help her find them."

"Can't the servants do that? For that matter, can't they do this sewing as well?" Maria surprised herself with the question. The African helpers travelling with them were wagon drivers, caring for the oxen or manoeuvring the heavy transports into position whenever they set up or dismantled camp.

"Maria! Whatever is the matter with you? It's not like you to be so churlish with your tasks. Go on, take a stool and sit in the sunshine over there, where there's a bit of a breeze." Tannie Susanna wafted a hand towards a clearing near the smouldering embers of the morning fire. "And don't let anyone know, but yes, of course someone else could catch the hens, but if I don't go out and see something other than the inside of this tent, I'll go mad."

With a wink, she gave Maria's shoulder a gentle tap before marching across the sludgy grass in the direction of Tannie Elisabeth and her chickens.

Maria closed one eye, her tongue poking out of the corner of her mouth as she threaded another length of cotton onto her needle. After their chat on the trek into Natal, Tannie Susanna's attitude had softened. Young as she was, Maria had become a friend to the grieving mother.. Oom Erasmus was properly old, but not Tannie Susanna. She liked the sensation of friendship, although remained wary, keeping her hopes for the future in check. Those she loved had a habit of leaving her.

"Ow." The needle pierced into the skin of her thumb. Maria threw the buttonless shirt onto the pile and rose from her stool.

The sun caught her in the eyes. Was that someone riding towards them? A shape shimmered in the distance. Maria's throat went dry. The shape grew closer, closer. A man. On a horse. Galloping as though chased by the enemy's hordes.

As the blurred outlines of the figure sharpened, Maria drew in a breath. The way the man sat upright in the saddle, not slouched like the farm boys. His hat pushed back from his forehead. George. What was he doing here?

She gathered her skirts and ran to him. He hauled on the reins, shouting at his horse to stop, at Maria to mind out. Hooves pounded through the squelching grass, nostrils flared, sweat flecked the animal's neck.

"Whoa. Maria, what are you doing? He'll trample you." George wheeled his horse in circles, calming him with tuts and clicks.

"What about you, George? What are you doing here?" Maria gripped the horse's bridle, pulled it to a halt. "Something's wrong, isn't it? I knew it. It hasn't felt right since yesterday. I thought it was just the storm passing over. But it isn't, is it?"

George slid from his saddle, covered her hand holding the bridle with his damp palm. His beard had thickened into an untidy tangle. Dark smudges under his eyes accentuated the impression of exhaustion evident in the slump of his shoulders.

"It was a massacre, Maria. Dingaan tricked Retief and his men. Invited them to a party and — " he wiped his mouth with the back of his free hand. Maria bit her lip to prevent crying out at the sudden pain as he tensed the other. " — clubbed them to death…"

"Oh…" The ground shifted beneath Maria's feet. She stumbled against George.

"Sorry. I should have found a kinder way to break the news."

Maria waved his concern away. "No, please, tell me the rest."

"There's not much else to tell. Not yet anyway." George looked away, as if searching the distant horizon. "There's going to be trouble. Dingaan is emboldened, and his impis will stop at nothing to drive us from their land. You'll have to learn to fight, little sister. And fight well."

The ground settled, hard and stable. Maria tugged on George's arm, made him look at her. "Impis. What are they?"

"Warriors. There's no other word to describe them. They may only wear animal skins and carry leather shields, but make no mistake. They are the best fighters I've ever seen." He blinked. "They're merciless."

"Were you there? At the…when it happened?"

"No. We were in the vicinity. Our scouts reported some strange goings-on, so Commandant Pretorious ordered us to be wary. He wanted us close enough to assist, but not so close we were tangled up in anything."

"Commandant Pretorius? You are still with his commando?" Her insides somersaulted..

"Yes, I've stayed with them since I left you — "

"And Christiaan Venter. Does he ride with you?" She held her breath. Why did her heart beat so fast?

"Oh, Maria." A shadow passed over George's face. But the sky remained cloudless.

"What? Is he…?"

"No, no. He's with the commando. We've been involved in some skirmishes. Clashes. He…"

"George. Stop mumbling. Tell me."

Kind, sad eyes searched her face. Could he read her as easily as Christiaan…? "George. Please."

"He was injured. A spear thrown by one of the impis. Caught him here — " fingers fluttered across her cheek " — there's a mark. A scar. He's not as…as handsome as you may remember him."

CHAPTER FIFTEEN

Sooilaer, South Africa. 7 February 1838

"Maria, I have to meet with Pa and Oom Gert." George dropped Maria's hand. "Will you be alright? Come with me. We'll find Ma, make sure you're with someone."

"What? Oh, no, there's no need. I'll walk back." Maria moved away. She plucked at her apron, bunching the fabric between her fingers. Injured. Disfigured. Alive. "You need to pass on the news to your father, of course."

"Commandant Pretorious is on his way here. He wants to use Sooilaer as a base, for the time being. The commando will need supplies, food…"

"He's coming here? With the whole commando? With everyone?"

"Yes." George hoisted himself into the saddle. "He sent me on ahead. They'll be here by nightfall."

He gathered the reins. His horse, calmed and nibbling the grass, responded with a stamp of a foot.

"Then you must hurry with your message. Your father is already with Oom Gert, at his wagon. He's been with him since breakfast. So the rumours of trouble were true. They must have known, somehow." Maria patted the horse's neck. "Don't worry about me, George. I'll find your mother, explain why you're here. She'll talk to the women, prepare them for whatever lies ahead. You know her. She's as good at organising her troops as Commandant Pretorious is his."

Her laugh rang false. George frowned, opened his mouth as though to speak, to persuade.

Maria slapped the horse's rump. "Go, George. I'll see you later."

George raised a hand in salute, flicked the horse into motion, and cantered towards the encircled wagons.

Maria watched his progress. So much to do, to plan, to organise. She needed to find Tannie Susanna, take her aside and warn her about George's return, about the commando. About the disaster they faced. Hurry! No time to waste. Run.

Her body refused to respond to her instructions, her muscles paralysed by a sapping weariness. The fog, so long absent, blanketed her with its heaviness. Perhaps she should lie down, curl up in the late afternoon sunshine and sleep.

"No, Maria, no." She pinched her cheeks, willing herself out of the haze. Now isn't for resting. She stumbled forward, concentrating on placing her feet with care so she didn't trip and fall. One step, two. Deep breath. Bite down on the panic. Run.

"Tannie Susanna!" Maria, breathless, her side aching and her cheeks burning, burst onto a scene of relaxed, laughing friendship. The circle of women beside Tannie Elisabeth's wagon froze at her sudden appearance, steaming mugs of coffee suspended in mid-air, their host pausing her story in surprise.

"Maria. Whatever is the matter? Where on earth have you been? Your dress is covered in mud." Tannie Susanna rose from her place amongst her companions. "My apologies, ladies. Maria here seems to have been chasing more than your hens, Elisabeth. I'm sorry to break up the party, but I think I should go with her to our tent, help her clean up."

Polite smiles, muttered assurances. Tannie Susanna gripped Maria's elbow, pulling her from the gathering. A twittering chatter of confused concern followed their departure.

Out of sight of the others, worry lines replaced the crinkles of a smile.

"What is it, Maria? Has something happened? You're in a dreadful state."

"George is here."

Tannie Susanna stopped in her tracks, her hand remaining on Maria's elbow, a flush of colour reddening her cheeks. "What do you mean, George is here? He can't be. He's with Andries and his commando. Far from here."

Maria shook her head. "No. He's here. Piet Retief is dead. All the men with him as well. The commando is on their way to Sooilaer, to resupply and set up camp. George says it won't be safe. We'll have to fight, he says." Maria's vision starred at a sudden rush of lightheadedness. She'd discharged her message. Further action was someone else's responsibility. "He's gone to inform Oom Erasmus and Oom Gert. He told me to fetch you, ask you to prepare the women for their arrival. They would be here by dusk, he said."

"Dusk?" Tannie Susanna glanced up at the sky. "That doesn't give us many hours. Did he say the number of men with him?"

Maria shook her head again.

"Are they bringing casualties? Were any of them hurt?" Tannie Susanna's expression softened. "Maria, is your friend with them?"

Maria touched the wooden cross at her neck. "George said they weren't attacked. Not this time. They kept their distance, he said." She fixed her attention on the lengthening shadows. How long before they got here? "Christiaan was injured sometime before. But he's alive, so that's what matters. Isn't it?"

A rainbow smile through falling tears.
***

Maria poked at the coals. Sparks danced in the air. The throb of her earlier headache had returned, not from the dull monotony of mending but the rush and scramble in response to George's arrival.

Oom Gert had called a council of war, as he termed it, gathering the men to his wagon to discuss the situation. Oom

Erasmus waited there, promising prayer and protection. So Tannie Susanna said. She'd bustled from one wagon to the next, organising the women into a busyness she argued would keep fear and grief from devouring them. Campfires were lit, pots of coffee brewed, meat roasted, bread baked.

Andries Pretorius rode into camp as the sun dipped below the distant Drakensberg mountains and the mist drifted in off the river. Oom Gert and Oom Erasmus greeted him and hurried him to their headquarters, while Maria and the other women watched from the shifting shadows of the firelight.

Parties of two or three emerged from the gloom, silent except for the huff and snort of worn-out horses. Women hurried forward, a mirror to the African servants waiting to lead exhausted beasts to water and fodder. Maria's heart jumped at each new arrival, only to sink into a thump of disappointment as the one rider she sought failed to appear.

Perhaps George was mistaken, and he was no longer with the group. Maybe his injury was more severe than anyone realised. She would delay retiring to bed for another few minutes. She threw a slim log onto the fire.

Please, Lord.

"Maria." The voice was deeper, rasping. Tired. A figure stepped from the shelter of the wagon.

Christiaan.

Maria ran to him, the emerging young woman abandoned to the excitement of the little girl greeting her playmate. She flung her arms around him. "You came. I looked for you, but you weren't in any of the groups I saw. I thought you had gone somewhere else, that George was wrong. He said you were injured."

Christiaan stiffened, prised her arms from around his neck. The orange glow of the flames illuminated one side of his face. The other remained shadowed. Hidden.

"I rode in from the other side. We had to make certain we weren't followed. This is the soonest I could get away. To find you." The searching Tannie Johanne eyes burrowed deep. "I wasn't sure if you would remember me."

"How could I forget you?" Maria lifted the necklace. "You left a piece of yourself with me."

Christiaan fingered the wooden carving. "You still wear it."

"Always."

He let the cross drop. Dug his fists into his overcoat pockets. Distanced himself with more than the single step backwards. "I left a piece of myself on a warrior's spear, too." He ducked his head. "How much did George tell you?"

Maria stepped into the growing gap between them. She itched to reach up, to turn his cheek into the light, to see. "Will you show me?"

"It isn't pretty, Maria."

"When was I bothered by pretty?"

He inhaled a long, shuddering breath. Lifting his head, he turned his face in a slow arc, his eyes closed.

Maria covered the gasp with hands clamped to her mouth. A red slash puckered the skin from the outer corner of his eye to the edge of his mouth. His lip curled upward in what looked like a snarl of anger.

"Does it hurt?" A whisper.

A shrug. Eyes still closed. "A bit. Less so than it did. The doctor says much of that side will go numb. Eventually."

"Can I touch it?"

His eyes flipped open, his body recoiling out of reach. "No! Why would you want to? It's…it's revolting."

A hint of nauseous revulsion churning Maria's insides dissolved at the glistening of tears in his eyes. She wasn't the only one whose heart wrote libraries. Pain, shame, disgust. As clear as the letters of her Bible.

"No, it isn't. It's a carving of the story of your absence. A story I want to read and share and understand." Her fingertip traced the pattern marring his cheek, hovered above the raw flesh.

He shifted his position the merest fraction. Rested his cheek against her palm. Allowed the salt of his pain to drip through her fingers.

Chapter Sixteen

Sooilaer, South Africa. August 1838

"Hold still, Christiaan." Maria smeared the sticky resin along the line of the scar, massaging its healing into Christiaan's damaged cheek. "Oh, but, am I hurting you?"

"No. I told you, the doctor said there'd be no feeling, no sensation within a few weeks of the injury." Christiaan trailed Maria's fingers down the puckered flesh. "And he was right. I don't even know it's my face I'm touching."

"It is getting better though, isn't it?" Maria circled the gloop around the edge of his upturned lip. She was sure it looked less severe, less taut. But was that wishful thinking?

Christiaan pulled her hand away. "Stop."

Maria shrunk from the crackle of aggression. "I'm sorry, I thought I was helping."

"We both know I'm stuck with this for life, no matter how much of your potion you plaster over me. It's a waste of time." He dropped her hand. "Of yours. And mine."

Maria's eyes widened at the rebuke. She busied herself with wrapping the aloe vera leaf into the damp cotton in which she stored it, her head bent over her task. She wouldn't let him read the hurt on her face, wouldn't allow the Tannie Johanne eyes to witness the cracking and breaking of her heart. She blinked away tears before they could fall.

The winter chill drifting in from the river seeped through the fabric of her dress, fingers of ice dancing on her skin and making her shiver.

"I'd best get back. Tannie Susanna will be looking for me." A grasshopper stalked through the grass at her feet, its emerald green armour bright against the parched carpet of brown. *We look like grasshoppers even to ourselves.* Where was her Joshua now?

A sigh. No, a groan. "No, it's me who is sorry, Maria. I didn't mean to upset you." The grasshopper paused. "Please, don't hurry away. You've done more for me these past months than I can ever thank you. Accepted me in the state I showed up in here. Scoured the river bank and the fields for remedies and salves to nurse me to health. You've even managed to hide how sickened you are at the sight of me. Well, almost…"

Her head snapped up. Grasshopper forgotten.

"I'm not sickened. I'm saddened." If only she could put into words the twist of sorrow every time Christiaan hid his face from her, turning away if she approached from his injured side. Remaining in the shadows of the firelight instead of joining the others in evening hymns and songs. The lines in her face, the tilt of her mouth or the flicker of her eyes no doubt spoke for her. But he misunderstood. Her grief wasn't for herself. "I feel so sorry for — "

"No! Not sorry for me, Maria, never that. I won't carry your pity with me when I leave."

"Leave? You didn't say…"

He fiddled with the top button of his mended overcoat, her neat stitches concealing the rips of battle. "I wanted to say a proper goodbye, give you a gift, assurances, something. But — "

That's what this was about; the mountain ride of his aggression, the slump into bitter despair. The truth whooshed upon Maria with the force of a springtime flood raging with the swollen waters of melted snow. A few months of rest, and he was healed enough to fight. The failed expedition in April of another commando, the creeping advance of Dingaan's warriors; he'd mentioned them in passing, when out working alongside her in the fields or chatting with George and Oom Erasmus over their evening meal.

How foolish. She'd thought his lonely rides, with his gun slung over his shoulder, were in search of peace and meat for the pot. That was practice, wasn't it? Getting fit for the rigours of war, far from the prying gaze of a nervous community.

"I wish you'd told me." A further thought, settling like a stone dropped from the rushing flow. You might not come back this time. Her fingers strayed to the necklace at her throat.

The sudden mocking 'piet-my-vrou' call of a cuckoo.

"Perhaps I should have done. I don't know. I didn't want to spoil everything." A lopsided grin. "I've enjoyed being here. With you."

The cuckoo fell silent.

"I will return, Maria. I'm certain of it."

"Don't say that, Christiaan. You can't be certain of anything." Maria folded her arms across her chest. Protecting her heart. "Except danger."

"And the goodness of the Lord, Maria. I can be sure of that." He untangled her hands. "I didn't tell you before. But I saw that spear fly through the air, right at me. Saw the whites of the eyes of the man who threw it. He hated me, for no other reason than that I was there in front of him. And all I could think, all I could hear, was your name. Maria. Waiting for me. Set aside for me. And I knew I was saved. For you."

The gun barrel wavered, the enamel cup used for target practice jiggling in and out of Maria's line of sight with every escaping giggle.

"Maria. You have to take this seriously." George reached an arm around, steadied the weapon. "You won't be laughing when it's the screaming face of an impi bearing down on you."

"Sorry, George. It feels so silly. I know they're somewhere, but we've seen nothing of these warriors you so fear anywhere near here. All this practising seems pointless. Could I aim at rabbits or something instead? At least that would be useful."

"And so will this prove to be. Useful, I mean. Try again. Drop your shoulders, you're all hunched." He pressed a hand onto her shoulder.

A fluttering butterfly-wish that Christiaan was her instructor.

"Right, take a breath, slow your heart rate down. Squeeze the trigger. Gently. If you pull too hard, you'll lose your line. And fire…"

A pop. The sharp pain of the rifle's recoil bruising her shoulder. Smoke blinding. Ears ringing. Ping.

"You did it. You hit your target. Look." George clapped her on the back. Brothers in arms.

Maria lowered the weapon, resting the butt on the ground. She wiped away the sting of the smoke, rubbed the lump on her shoulder. "Ow. How do you do this over and over, George? You must be black and blue by the time a battle is over. And not only from the spears or whatever it is that get thrown at you."

"You get used it, learn to anticipate the backlash." George gave her a sympathetic pat. Much the way she'd seen him pat his horse after a hard ride. "But you haven't looked at your handiwork. See? Enemy down, Maria."

The cup lay on its side in the grass, dented and misshapen.

"Tannie Susanna won't be happy about her coffee cup, George. Enemy or not." Laughter gurgled.

"You should laugh more often, sussie. It makes you prettier." George grinned. "Just not when you're trying to shoot straight."

Maria punched his arm, the bubbling laughter escaping in full-throated delight.

"You've been different these last few weeks." George raised an enquiring eyebrow. "Anything you want to tell your adopted big brother? You know, about a certain young man and a promise he may have made?"

The laughter tinged with guilt. Maria wished she could tell him her secret.

"It's good you're still here, George." She hoped her praise would distract him from further questions.

"Not for much longer. Commandant Pretorius can't fight all the battles without a full complement of men. You understand that. More than most of the women, I suspect."

Maria shivered, all amusement blown like chaff on the wind. She raised the rifle, wedging it in place in the hollow of her shoulder. "Choose another target for me, George. I want to be ready."

# CHAPTER SEVENTEEN

Sooilaer, South Africa. September, 1838

"Susanna. Wake up, Susanna. You have to come."

Maria rolled onto her side. Still dark. She burrowed further under the covers. Tannie Isobel. In their tent, in the middle of the night. She was dreaming.

"Susunna. it's urgent. Your brother..."

Oom Gert? Wide awake. A covered candle bobbed across the tent. Held aloft by Tannie Isobel.

Maria struggled upright, rubbing the sleep from her eyes.

"Tannie Isobel? Is that you? What are you doing here?" She kept her voice to a whisper. No need to alarm everyone if this was a mistake.

"Maria, I didn't mean to disturb you. It's Susanna I need. She must hurry. Oom Gert isn't well."

Maria's throat tightened from more than sleep-disturbed thirst. "His fever? Has it got worse?"

"Yes. I sent Susanna away yesterday evening, told her to get some rest. He was quite stable when she left."

"Isobel? Maria? What's going on?" Susanna emerged from her corner of the tent, draping a shawl over her shoulders. Tendrils of hair escaped from the cotton headscarf she wore at night.

"Susanna..." Isobel skirted the crate they used as a table, her candle sweeping the ground with its light. "I'm sorry to disturb your rest. But you should come. Gert is...troubled. He's calling for you."

Susanna slumped forward, grasping at a chair for support. "You should have let me stay, Isobel." Her voice distant, faint.

"I knew it was his time. The Lord calling him away, so he wouldn't have to endure our humiliation, our defeat."

Isobel hooked the lantern over a length of rope dangling from the canvas roof. "Maria, fetch a drink of water. And gather some clothes for Susanna. You'll have to walk with us, help me support her across to the Oom Gert's quarters."

Maria threw off the bedcovers, grabbing for her coat to pull over her nightgown. She retrieved a canteen of water, kept warm in a basket of hay covered in blankets. A necessary precaution to prevent ice forming during the cooler months Handing it to Tannie Isobel, she tiptoed to Tannie Susanna's sleeping area.

Oom Erasmus lay on his back, his mouth slack and his thinning hair sticking out at odd angles on the pillow.

"What if I wake him?" She turned to Tannie Isobel, uncertain. A grunting snore offered reassurance.

"He won't stir until the first cock crows, Maria. Collect what's needed, and let's go."

Her breath steamed in the frigid winter air. Stars sprinkled the velvet blue of the sky with their diamond twinkles. A jackal barked, hunting somewhere along the banks of the river.

Tannie Susanna, wrapped in an overcoat belonging to Oom Erasmus, and boots of Maria's shoved onto her feet, shuffled through the frost-crunching grass, Tannie Isobel and Maria looping an arm on either side.

News must have travelled about Oom Gert's worsening condition. Women stood in small groups at the entrance to his tent. His servants piled logs onto an already blazing fire. Muted conversations fell silent as Tannie Susanna approached, heads bowed in respect.

"We are praying for his swift release, Susanna dearest." An older woman, indistinguishable in the pale moonlight.

Maria held her breath. Was release what Tannie Susanna sought for her brother? Perhaps the woman meant release from the grip of fever and nothing more.

They ducked into the tent.

Oom Gert's covers lay in a rumpled heap at the end of the bed. Any attempt by the nurse assigned to his care to replace them resulted in a wild, wide-eyed thrashing of arms and legs, his head tossing from side to side on the pillow.

Tannie Susanna rushed to his side, her need for assistance forgotten. "It's alright, Gert, I'm here. It's Susanna." She reached for the covers. "No wonder he doesn't want these on him. They're drenched in sweat and stinking. Fetch some fresh covers. You can go to my wagon."

Maria rose to run the errand. Tannie Isobel gripped her arm. "Not you, Maria. The nurse shall go. And rouse Erasmus too. His services will be required before the sun's up."

Tannie Susanna held a cup to her brother's lips, whispering an encouragement to drink.

"How do you know? He could recover, couldn't he? He's been this sick any number of times before."

Tannie Isobel shook her head. "Not this time, dear. Hear that breathing? He's not much longer for this world."

"But what will we do? Who will lead us?" Maria spoke louder than intended, panic forcing its presence into her words. She held her shawl over her mouth. "Sorry. It's just — there's no one else, is there?"

"Shh, that's not a discussion for now. Oom Gert will have thought of that. He knows his health has been ailing. It's been obvious to anyone who bothered to look." Had Maria bothered? She wasn't sure. Caught up with caring for Christiaan, enjoying developing her rifle skills, helping George prepare for his return to the commando; when had she thought Oom Gert's stooped walk, or his watery eyes, or his tired speech was anything more than normal?

"Did Tannie Susanna know?" A prickle of guilt. "I should have seen, shouldn't I? Helped her prepare. After Salomon, and everything."

"Ah, you're only a child, Maria. No, don't take offence. You have other worries, other concerns, than the plight of a weakened old man." Tannie Isobel patted her arm. "You have a future with a healthy — and still handsome, despite what he says — young man to think about."

A blush warmed Maria's cheeks despite the chill billowing in from the tent's entrance. She pulled her bonnet lower over her face. Perhaps Tannie Isobel wouldn't notice.

Oom Erasmus raised his hands to heaven. "And so, Lord, we commit this, your servant, into your care. We thank you for his leadership and courage throughout our pilgrimage. We trust you to carry him into the promised land of your presence even as you continue to take us left on earth on our journey to freedom. Amen."

"Amen." The congregation responded with quiet, saddened voices.

Beside Maria, Tannie Susanna shivered, regardless of the hot, dry wind blowing in from the mountains, and the shawl she hugged tight.

"Let's get you back, Susanna. You're not well." Tannie Elisabeth tucked an arm around Tannie Susanna's waist.

Sweat beaded on Tannie Susanna's forehead, the pallor of her skin accentuated by bruised smudges under her eyes, the flush of feverish colour on her cheeks. She seemed not to hear, not to notice Tannie Elisabeth's gentle touch. Her lips moved in silent — prayer? Distress?

"He can't stay here." The whisper like leaves sighing in the nearby trees. "They'll discover his grave. Desecrate it."

"You'll discuss that with Erasmus later." Tannie Elisabeth spoke with the firm authority of a parent to a troubled child. "Maria, run on ahead and prepare some tea and a bed for Susanna. She can rest in the shade of your wagon for the remainder of today. I'll make sure no one disturbs her."

Maria hurried away, grateful for the excuse to leave yet another gravesite. Death and tragedy, that's all this journey led to. No promised land. No divine protection. A vision of a ruined face, a spear hurled from the hands of a demented enemy — now a regular actor in the nightmares tangling her bedclothes and waking her with moans uttered from parched lips.

Their deserted camp echoed the desolation of Tannie Susanna's resurgence of grief. A stool lay sideways in the grass, knocked over by the violence of a gust of wind. Powdery ashes rose from the uncleared remains of an earlier fire. A crow scavenged for scraps in the grass.

"Shoo, shoo." Maria flapped her hands at the bird. It squawked in indignant protest, retreating to the nearby bushes from where it eyed her with wary interest. Clearing the fireplace of yesterday's debris, she piled sticks of kindling into a pyramid, struck the flint firestarter to elicit a few sparks and set light to the bundle of dried grasses she added to the twigs. Orange flames leapt upward, the wind catching them and igniting the brushwood within seconds. Maria took a few minutes to feed the infant fire with thicker branches and logs until a satisfying crackle and smell of wood smoke filled the air.

Keeping an eye on the blaze, Maria spooned dried and shredded red bush leaves into the enamel teapot. She filled it with water from a container and wedged it in place over the glowing coals, remaining on her knees at the fireside. Attracted to its warmth.

What would happen to the community now? Who would lead them? Had anyone even heard of Oom Gert's death beyond the boundary of their encircled wagons? Thoughts and worries scurried through her mind like the rats she'd scared from the rubbish pit outside the camp. Gnawing at her peace, chewing at her fragile faith in a God who saw and knew. And cared.

"Tannie Johanne, I hope you pray for us. I'm not sure we pray for ourselves anymore. Or believe anyone answers. Is the

Lord with you, as you promised He would be? God, did you stay behind, with only enough love to spare for one old lady? Or do You camp here, too?" The words poured out in a tumble of whispered anguish.

"I'm glad to see you praying, child." Tannie Isobel's appearance startled Maria. She scrabbled to her feet, adjusting her bonnet and smoothing her apron.

"I wasn't praying. I wouldn't know how to. Not like Oom Erasmus tells us to." She busied herself with the boiling teapot, trying to hide her discomfort at being discovered talking to herself.

"Oh, you don't have to pray all those long and formal prayers of his, Maria." Tannie Isobel collected cups from a box beside the wagon, brought them to the makeshift table. "I saw Elisabeth walking with Susanna from the service. I thought you might want some help. Here. And speaking whatever is on your heart, in whatever words you have, is the prayer I believe the Lord likes to listen to. It's a bit less fussy and fancy."

An impish smile flashed. Maria swallowed her astonishment. Never in all their previous conversations, her visits to knit with Debora, or tea parties with Tannie Susanna, had Tannie Isobel spoken with such irreverence.

The woman laughed. "Don't look so shocked. My mother grew up with Andrew Murray as her pastor. You may not have heard of him — he came from Scotland many years ago. He encouraged his congregation to talk to God as though He were a friend. Ma taught me to do the same." She squeezed Maria's shoulder. "It helps, with everything else so uncertain. God sees and cares more than we realise."

Maria blinked. Her scurrying fear answered in a throwaway comment as Tannie Isobel poured tea. Perhaps someone was listening even to her unspoken thoughts. Did that comfort — or terrify — her?

CHAPTER EIGHTEEN

Wasbank, South Africa. 9 December 1838

"Our Father who art in heaven,
Hallowed be thy name.
Thy kingdom come, Thy will be done,
On earth as it is in heaven
Give us this day our daily bread;
And forgive us our debts,
As we also have forgiven our debtors;
And lead us not into temptation,
But deliver us from evil. Amen."

The stout figure of Pastor Cilliers raised his arms heavenward as the assembled congregation echoed his closing refrain. The mid-morning sun emerged from behind a cloud, its rays slanting in golden acceptance of their prayer.

A thrill of anticipation shivered through Maria. Ever since Andries Pretorius' commissioning two weeks previously as the Commander-in-Chief of the Voortrekkers in Natal, frenetic preparations for a major offensive against Dingaan and his impis replaced the stupor of grief over the community at Sooilaer. Under the guidance of an emissary from a headquarters deeper in the region's interior, they had prepared fifty-seven wagons for moving to the fighting front, building new protective gates to slot into the gaps left by the commandeered wagons.

Days at Tannie Susanna's bedside, calming her cries and soothing the heat of a fever similar to her brother's, caused Maria to doubt the broken woman would ever return to her former dynamic self. But it seemed the stimulus of a proposed move away from the scene of tragedy reignited her leadership. She strode from one wagon to the next, instructing and coordinating the packing of supplies, or arranging protection for the younger children and older women remaining behind during the campaign. She urged Oom Erasmus to resume daily prayer gatherings, spent evenings scribbling in her diary by the light of campfire and candle.

To Maria, this commissioning service offered a fresh start, a blank page for the journal of her life. Pastor Cilliers strode up and down the elevated platform, a Bible balanced in one hand. In his other, he waved a white handkerchief, using it to wipe his glistening face at each change in direction.

"Though we are small in number, yet, as with Gideon and the Israelites when they confronted the hordes of Midian, we need not fear the outcome of our battles."

"The Book of Judges." Tannie Susanna squeezed Maria's hand. "I was reading it the other day. Victory belongs to the Lord, Maria."

"Shh." Oom Erasmus frowned across at them.

"If we determine to turn our attention to the Almighty and seek His guidance, His instruction, we are assured of His miraculous salvation." Pastor Cilliers thumped the Bible with his fist. "The men standing before us today need our prayers. And our commitment."

A shuffling of feet as the front rows of men straightened their shoulders.

"Will you join me in making a vow together? A vow to stand as witness to the rescuing power of God, for ourselves and for our children's children."

The hairs on Maria's arms tingled as a hush fell over the assembly. Someone near the back coughed. The breeze held its breath.

Pastor Cilliers faced his audience. Closing his Bible with slow, deliberate movements, he raised it aloft. Maria thought he closed his eyes, but couldn't be certain from her position behind other, taller congregants. She would rise on tiptoe for a better view but feared Oom Erasmus' displeasure.

The pastor cleared his throat.

"Here we stand before the holy God of heaven and earth, to make a vow to Him that, if He will protect us and give our enemy into our hand, we shall keep this day and date every year as a day of thanksgiving like a sabbath, and that we shall erect a house to His honour wherever it should please Him, and that we also will tell our children that they should share in that with us in memory for future generations. For the honour of His name will be glorified by giving Him the fame and honour for the victory."

The waves of his words crashed over Maria, somersaulting her in a confusion of emotions. The dark face of her nightmares; the pop of a rifle; the remembered acrid smell of cordite. A graveside and a burial, embroidered flowers and Tannie Johanne's circling strokes of comfort between her shoulders. A spear and a scar. And a cross carved in wood hanging from her neck.

She fidgeted to see between the rows of bowed heads. There was George, hands in pockets, chin lifted. He would be staring ahead, mouthing the spoken words and committing them to memory. A smile of affection. How fond she had grown of her brother over the winter and spring.

Next to him, a shaggy tangle of blond hair, freckled neck. Sunburnt ears.

Then a grey head streaked with white. The dirty collar of his shirt turned up.

A flutter of her pulse. A slide of her insides. Dark hair curled against the leather-brown skin of his neck.

He adjusted his stance. Could he feel her eyes on him? A slight turn of the head. A cheek marred by a furrow of white.

CHAPTER NINETEEN

Banks of the Buffalo River, South Africa. 16 December, 1838

"Maria, you're with me." Christiaan's voice carried over the hubbub.

He strode through the circle of wagons without waiting to see if she followed, his expectation clear that she should. He gripped a rifle in each hand; twin bandoliers criss-crossed his shoulders. No longer the playmate of youth, this was the soldier marching to the fight.

Maria hurried to catch up with him, lifting her skirts from dragging through the wet grass. The mist of the previous evening draped the pre-dawn shadows with its cloak of damp, a raw breeze billowing in from the river.

"Wait, Christiaan. Where are we going?"

Christiaan paused, looked over his shoulder. "To fight, Maria. Hurry. We must be in position before sunrise."

Maria's heart flipped. "Me? I have to take a weapon and shoot?"

She hadn't thought that the plan as they trundled out of Wasbank, wagons laden with the equipment of war, Andries Pretorious leading the way. Pastor Cilliers accompanied the convoy, his daily services and prayers reminding them all of their promise to honour God once He secured them certain victory over Dingaan's warriors. The women travelling with the group — Tannie Susanna, Tannie Elisabeth, and even Tannie Isobel amongst them — were not going to be called upon to do battle, but rather offer the commando support from a distance. So Maria had believed.

"No, of course not." Christiaan resumed his march as she reached his side. "These rifles take too long to load between firings. I'll be an easy target if I do that myself. You'll help me."

"Oh, yes, I can do that." Relief released in a giggle. Recollections of lessons with George, prodding and poking the barrel of his gun, him timing how long she took. She'd wondered why he was so obsessed — and impressed — with her speed.

"No, this isn't funny." The muscles of Christiaan's jaw clenched, the scar standing out in stark relief on a flushed cheek. He stopped, whirled around to confront Maria, anger burning in the gentle Tannie Johanne eyes. "This is war. Unsafe, unkind, desperate war. You will see things today you will never wash from your memory, no matter how hard you try. You will hear things which will wake you in the silence of night long after today is over. You — " his breath caught. "I should never have asked you. It was foolish of me to want…"

Maria, a vague unease stirring, resisted her initial reaction to bite back against his dismissal. "To want what, Christiaan? Tell me."

"To want you at my side during this thing. To have you understand what it's like, see for yourself what George, what the others, endure." He hung his head. "What I go through."

Any remaining laughter drained from Maria at his mumbled confession.

"Is it really that awful?" Her head guessed at realities; for the first time, her heart did as well. "None of you ever say anything. Andries Pretorious, when he rides to declare your victories; George. You."

Christiaan fingered his cheek. "It robs a man of all that is human." He shuddered. "But look, the sky lightens and dawn is upon us. We need to ready our positions. Is this too heavy for you?" He held out a rifle.

Maria balanced the weight in her hand, adjusting her hold on the barrel until it felt comfortable. "No. George made me carry his out to the fields whenever he took me for practice. Now I know why."

"A good man, George." Christiaan grabbed her free hand, squeezed her fingers. "He's prepared you well. And I will trust that the Lord has, too. May we have the victory this day. And may you continue by my side until we do."

Christiaan handed Maria his fired weapon, grabbed the reloaded one from her without looking, his attention fixed on the screeching mass of bare-chested warriors across the water.

"Watch out!"

A spear thumped into the soft sand a few yards from the wagon where Maria sheltered. The crack of rifle fire in response. A gurgling cry.

Maria fumbled with burnt, blistered fingertips to reload the rifle stock. She resumed the hymn she hummed, desperate to drown out the terrifying sounds of battle filling the air. She inhaled through her mouth in short, shallow breaths, trying not to taste the repugnant smell drifting from the riverbank.

Rifle swap.

This was beyond anything she imagined. The nightmare appearance of Christiaan's imaginary attacker was a childish caricature compared to this reality.

Rifle swap.

A wisp of smoke curled from the spent barrel. She blinked against the searing pain of another burn, biting her lip to prevent the scream of hysteria escaping.

"They're regrouping." Christiann slumped next to her. Sweat streaked his face, camouflaging the scar with grime. He removed his hat. Damp curls clung to his forehead. He fanned himself with the crumpled headgear. "We should get water, while there's a lull in the fighting. Have some food."

"Are we winning?" Maria licked parched lips with a thickened tongue. Water, yes. Food, no. Her stomach clenched against a roll of nausea at the thought. She might never eat again. "Oh, you're hurt. There's blood. On your neck."

Christiaan pressed a palm to his skin. "It's nothing. A scratch. From a stone or something. When that spear landed." He closed his eyes. Under the dirt, his skin looked pale.

"Are you sure? Let me look. I can clean it for you…"

"Leave it. There'll be more, before the day's out. Let's get a drink." Christiaan pushed to his feet, extended a hand for Maria.

Leg muscles stiff and awkward from crouching in the grass, Maria winced as she stood. "I'll manage. Thanks." If he refused her help, well, she would refuse his.

"To arms, men. The final attack has started." A shout from the Commander-in-Chief's position in the centre of the laager forestalled any thoughts of quenching their thirst. "Light the gun."

Maria flinched as a screeching whistle pierced the volleys of rifle fire, the shouts of raging impis. A distant thud rumbling through the ground, thumping like a monstrous heart beat.

Cheers.

"What…what was that?" She clutched at the collar of her dress.

"The field gun. Pretorius had it brought here, made ready for use in the event of a clear shot."

Another whistle. Another thud.

"It seems he found one." Christiaan grinned.

"It's hardly fair…"

Christiaan snatched his hand away, stared at her with flashing eyes, the grin a thin line of fury. "Fair? Is it fair that I have only half a face? Is it fair that Piet Retief was clubbed to death? Or that Hendrik Potgieter's expedition was ambushed, and Piet Uys and his son butchered?" He rammed his hat on his head. "And what about the women their sacrifice has saved? Women like you, Maria. Is it fair that you should live, and they die?"

Shoulders rigid, he grabbed his rifle from the ground.

"Go back to Tannie Susanna, Maria. We're finished here." He turned his back on her.

"We have them on the retreat." Andries Pretorius' triumphant shout prevented Maria from defending herself. "George, Hendrik. Saddle your horses and ride with me. We mustn't let them escape. Christiaan. You too. Hurry."

Without a word, Christiaan jogged to where the horses waited. He flung himself into the saddle of a dappled pony, a rifle slung over his shoulder. He whipped the reins, galloping out of the laager with a dozen other men.

What had she done? Would she ever see him alive, make right her mistake?

Through the gaps between the wagons, she glimpsed the scattering figures of Dingaan's men. Watched as puffs of gunfire rose from the rifles of galloping horsemen. Gagged for air as the waters of the river between its banks flowed red.

CHAPTER TWENTY

Pietermaritzburg, South Africa. 1839-1842

Berg Street
Pietermaritzburg
16 December 1839

Dearest Tannie Johanne

What can I say? Two years and not a word passed between us. How strange for me.

I hear that you're well and that the cottage is surrounded by flowers. As it should be. New arrivals give us news from the south. They tell of the effects of British rule, how the way of life changed beyond what is tolerable. The other day, Oom Marthinus visited us here at the house in Berg Street. You know him — the butcher who lived on the other side of Graaff-Reinet (it was he who mentioned your health and the flowers).

Tannie Susanna appeared most flustered when he called, as though he was an unexpected — unwanted? — guest. But I'm sure I saw her writing the invitation to him. I may be mistaken. But she hasn't been the same since this last year and the great Battle of Blood River. Did you know that's what everyone is calling it?

Her spirits revived in the first months after the victory, and I think she enjoyed planning our removal to the town at Pietermaritzburg. I know she felt proud that Oom Gert will be forever remembered in its name. She said so often enough. And, of course, poor Piet Retief is included. She was most affected by her brother's death, following so soon after Salomon's, and I began to wonder if she might ever recover.

As I say, the early months here restored the colour to her cheeks. She went about the town, taking tea with the other ladies, helping them to establish their new homes, set their affairs in order. That sort of thing.

I think she is unhappy with Oom Erasmus. I shouldn't say that really, should I? But you are my first confidante, Tannie Johanne, and my heart will always leak through my lips (or in this case, my pen) when I talk to you. In public, she remains at his side, loyal and submissive. She amens all his prayers and writes notes during his sermons. But at home, she withdraws to her desk under the window of the sitting room for hour after hour (Oom Erasmus occupies the only other spare room, which he uses for his study. He is more at home with his books than he is with his wife, I think). Tannie Susanna often shoos me from the room. She says she's praying and recording her thoughts in a sort of diary. But I have walked past the closed door and heard the sound of muffled crying many times.

Please pray for her. And for Oom Erasmus. I know you do, but I shall ask it, anyway. What is it the Lord says? "Ask and you will receive"? I am asking, and trust I receive.

Later this afternoon, Pastor Cilliers is holding a service to commemorate last year's victory. Some are calling today Dingaan's Day, and have called for every settler to celebrate it each year. Oom Erasmus says it should be reserved for solemn prayer and remembrance, but Tannie Susanna disagrees, saying a party uplifts the spirits of those who have endured the hardships of life since starting out on this Great Trek. I like her idea best. Although there is also much to reflect on.

I wonder what you would suggest if you were here? How I wish you were.

Andries Pretorius and his 'victory commando' continue to ride out against the Zulu king Dingaan. Everyone thought the battle would see him defeated, but he continues to defy all attempts to negotiate or allow us portions of his land. To further complicate matters, the British have established a presence at the harbour of Port Natal and are refusing to allow us access to its waters.

I hear all this from the many visitors received by Oom Erasmus. He remains an important figure in the community.

Did you hear that George left us? He joined the commando when we were still at Sooilaer. Relations between him and Tannie Susanna grew so bitter, I fear he will not return to us. He will never be Salomon, no matter how hard he tries. Even when Oom Andries brings his troops to the base here, George is not amongst them.

Another friend of his, Field-Cornet Christiaan Venter, also stays away. I fear I offended him at our last meeting. How I wish I could sit in the little chair you kept beside the hearth for me, drinking warm milk and eating the rusks you baked. I could tell you everything, and you would give me your wisdom and guidance.

Silly, I would no longer fit in the chair — if you even still have it. Nor do I like heated milk!

Oh, I completely forgot. Tannie Margarita and the clock! How could you not have told me I might meet her? She became my comforter and confidante in your absence before we travelled down into Natal. She spoke about your life before Graaff-Reinet. And somehow she helped me settle a few things about Ma and Pa. Not that she said anything in particular. Perhaps it was the link with Ma's home.

And then the clock. Do you remember it? Tannie Margarite said she'd kept it in the hope she would meet me some day and be able to carry out Ma's wishes, to give it to her children. And imagine, there were notes written by Ma when she was just a girl. I haven't deciphered much of the handwriting — it is very small and the ink has faded on the old paper. But having them makes me feel as if Ma is with me, somehow. Is that very strange?

I have enclosed a sample of embroidery worked by my young pupil, Debora. As you can guess, she is not a natural at needlework, but she improves with practice. Much practice! You would laugh to see how her tongue sticks out as she concentrates. And how often she pricks her finger and we have to soak spots of blood from her handiwork. I always enjoy her company and relish the time spent with her.

One day I hope to fulfil my promise, and fetch you to be with me here. I can imagine nothing more wonderful than that we establish a home together, growing flowers in the summer and perfecting my embroidery in winter. And talking all the while.

Until then, dearest Tannie Johanne, I pray for your continued health and strength. I hope the Lord hears my prayers as I know He does yours. I remain undecided if He has journeyed with us, or if He remains only by your side. If only one is permitted, I pray He would be with you.

With all my love, Maria

P.S. Please take the enclosed dried posy of local flowers to, well, you know where. And wish them my love.

Berg Street
Pietermaritzburg
16 December, 1840

Dear George

How can you have kept your courtship with Katerina a secret until now, when you announce your impending marriage to her? What a dreadful brother you are. I have spent hours examining the portrait you sent and conclude you are very lucky indeed to have caught the eye of so beautiful a woman. I believe I caught a glimpse of her the day of the battle. There was a young lady there assisting you. Am I right?

I'm sorry to admit your mother did not receive the news with the delight I would have wished for you. As she read your note, her lips puckered in that sour-lemon way they do sometimes. And her cheeks became very flushed. Indeed, for a brief moment, I feared she suffered from a relapse of the fever which so threatened her health at Sooilaer. I needn't have worried — and nor must you — as she regained her composure within a minute or two.

Your father, on the other hand, was exuberant in his delight when she handed him the card. He choked on his coffee, he was so moved. He leapt from his chair and began pacing our small parlour, declaring he must begin preparing for the wedding service with all haste, planning when and how you should return, declaring his undying affection for a future daughter he, as yet, hadn't met.

He left the room when your mother pointed out the invitation stated you would marry on the other side of the Drakensberg and not in our new Natalia Republic.

I'm sorry, I hope this doesn't cause you distress. I would love to travel to be with you both, but, as you are aware, it is too dangerous to travel alone. You and I shall have to plan a journey at a later date. Maybe when you have your first child?!

On a different note, do you not find it wonderful that we have finally established a community here? And have given ourselves the name of Republic? The British authorities don't yet recognise it as such, but I hear from your father that negotiations are ongoing. The new parliament seems very chaotic, with a decision made one day and reversed the next. Perhaps it all works better than I realise.

We haven't yet built the 'house of the Lord' we vowed to establish. Two years seems a long time to fulfil our promise when God delivered us so spectacularly, don't you think?

George, do you have word of Christiaan? I hate to ask, but cannot rest easy, not knowing how he fares. We are all delighted that Commandant Pretorius and your commando have overthrown Dingaan and formed a truce or alliance with his successor. (Were you involved in those campaigns, by the way?). They held a parade here in Pietermaritzburg to celebrate another victory, and some fighters were present. I thought I saw Christiaan, but, if it was him, he didn't acknowledge me. It saddens me to know I have damaged our friendship — for it was a friendship, wasn't it? — with an unthoughtful comment which it seems I can in no way apologise for.

Now don't laugh at your foolish little sister, but if you do meet Christiaan, please pass my fondest regards to him. Tell him I am truly sorry, and hope for the day when we can again be friends. Tell him I still wear the necklace. Every day.

I must end here, dearest George. The afternoon service of The Vow starts in the next hour and I have to help your mother prepare a light meal for guests she has invited. It will be a treat having the house filled with happiness and laughter, even if only for an evening.

Wishing you all the best with your preparations. Please give my love to your darling Katerina. I welcome her as a sister into my heart.

All my love brother, Maria

Berg Street
Pietermaritzburg
16 December, 1841

George!
I don't know what you said, but thank you. Christiaan visited us!

It was earlier in the year, and he didn't stay for long. Said he was paying a courtesy call to Oom Erasmus and Tannie Susanna (he didn't mention me) while he was passing through from Durban. He filled our small sitting room with his fidgety presence, preferring to stand, so he said, than make himself comfortable in a chair. Oom Erasmus persuaded him to stay for a cup of coffee, but even that he drank without sitting.

Is that something you learn to do when on campaign with Commandant Pretorius?

He is looking well. Christiaan, I mean. The scar doesn't appear as obvious as it used to. I suppose that's natural, with the passage of three years. He is just as I remembered him, with kind eyes that always reminded me of Tannie Johanne. Do you remember her, George? I do miss her, although your parents are kind to me, in their own way. I begin to think I should seek a home of my own, but without a husband — or prospect of one — I am doomed to live out my days enduring the hospitality of others.

Perhaps I could live with you and Katerina. Not as family — I would never presume that — but as nurse to your dearest baby boy. He sounds a delight, judging from your letters.

Dear George, I don't really hate it here. Christiaan's visit unsettled me, that's all. I don't know what I expected when Oom Erasmus ushered him into the house. He seemed so awkward and stiff, as if his visit were an unpleasant duty. He didn't seem to notice my presence at first, but then I caught him glancing my way while Oom Erasmus interrogated him as to the state of affairs elsewhere. I'm almost certain he winked at me, a tiny flick of his eyelid. I could feel the blush in my hair, George, and didn't dare look at your mother.

She gave me the one opportunity to talk to Christiaan, instructing me to take his cup and show him to the door. I could have hugged her. But didn't, of course.

We had only a few moments on the doorstep, but it was enough to reassure me Christiaan has forgiven my blunder. When I tried to apologise, he shushed me before the words left my lips. Instead, it was he apologising to me — for not writing, for not visiting. He explained, all in a rush, that his duties continued to take him elsewhere but that it was at your insistence that he should visit on his next excursion near Pietermaritzburg.

"And I see George was right. You still wear that little wooden cross. I'm glad."

That's what he said before leaving. It might be my imagination, but I sensed he was sad at our parting.

So whatever you said, it worked. Thank you.

I trust your Dingaan's Day celebrations are wonderful and your son enjoys hearing the stories of our deliverance for the first time.

All my love, Maria

Berg Street
Pietermaritzburg
16 December, 1842

Dearest Tannie Johanne

Another Day of the Vow, another year! Life is settling into a pattern here in Pietermaritzburg. Oom Erasmus spends most of his day in his study, as before. He receives fewer visitors now though. His hearing is failing, and I see it tires him to concentrate on the conversations of others for lengthy periods of time.

In contrast, Tannie Susanna is rarely home. She has gathered a group of ladies around her, and they meet regularly for Bible study and prayer, as well as tea and gossip. I have been once or twice, but they are mostly older than me, and so I feel somewhat excluded.

She has no contact with poor George, which saddens me. He has become less religious, less pious than she would like, and so this adds another bitter pill to those she already swallows. I write to him regularly though, passing on whatever family news there is to tell. I have asked him to bring his wife Katerina and their young son — did I mention they'd had a baby? — for a visit, but he seems to skip over those parts of my letters.

I will keep trying. 'Blessed are the peacemakers'. Isn't that what you always say?

Oh, Tannie Johanne, I am avoiding telling you my biggest news. Even as I write, my heart thumps in my chest in a most uncomfortable manner. No, I am not sick. Not in the way you may think, anyway.

Do you remember me telling you about Field-Cornet Christiaan Venter, from Commandant Pretorious' commando? Well, I'm not the only one taking on the role of peacemaker. Can you guess who? You never will.

George! I'm sure you didn't guess him.

I mentioned to him in an earlier letter that I regretted what I said to Christiaan at the Battle of Blood River, and how I wished for him to pass on my heartfelt apologies. They are in the same commando — I believe I told you — and so they know each other.

Anyway, he did exactly that. Christiaan visited for the first time last year. That was awkward, as you can guess. But now he calls whenever he is in the area. In fact, I think he might make a detour sometimes, with the express purpose of coming here to Berg Street. He declares he comes to update Oom Erasmus on the latest happenings in the region, bring Tannie Susanna fruit or cheese from his travels. But he always treats me with especial affection, commenting on my latest piece of needlepoint or the way I happen to wear my hair.

Tannie Susanna does not leave us alone for longer than our brief farewells at the front door, so please don't be alarmed on that score. And he has made no declaration of anything other than friendship. Yet.

He reminds me so much of you, Tannie Johanne. He has eyes as dark as pebbles, like yours. And he reads me as easily as I trust you are reading this letter. Which is sometimes a great thrill, and sometimes a great cause for alarm. He is kind and gentle, despite being a fighter and a soldier. I have seen him when his fury is piqued, though, and believe he does battle with much skill and success.

Here's the thing. He told me last time he was here that he might resign his commission soon. What do you think that could mean? Do you think I dare dream it has something to do with me? Or am I being foolish, running away with my imagination the way I used to chase after butterflies? The fog of old has not drifted across my thoughts for many months, but I feel its creeping presence as I confess these things to you.

I should stop, and trust in your love and prayers for me, to wait for the plan you say God has for me to unfold as naturally as a flower opens in spring.

How I will try!

I will write again as soon.

With all my love, Maria

CHAPTER TWENTY-ONE

Pietermaritzburg, South Africa. 4 August 1842

"The government in London has agreed to the petitions of the English settlers and is to grant Natal the status of a colony under British rule."

Blood bubbled on the tip of Maria's finger as the needle slipped in surprise at Oom Erasmus' dramatic entrance. The glassware on the shelf beside the door rattled in protest.

"Erasmus. Do you have to barge in so?" Tannie Susanna frowned at her work spread on the desk. "Look what you've made me do. I'll have to start this letter all over again. Anyway, what did you say?"

"I think it's you who are becoming hard of hearing, my dear, not me. I said, the British government — "

"Yes, yes, I heard the words. But what do they mean, Erasmus?"

Oom Erasmus sighed into the nearest armchair. He tapped a sheet of paper held in his left hand. "Exactly what I say. The British are to declare the whole region of Natal a colony, under their direct rule and protection. Apparently, they will endeavour to accommodate some of our more pressing stipulations, whilst refusing others."

"Let me see that." Tannie Susanna stretched forward. Taking the page, she tilted it into the light of afternoon sunshine dappling the parlour. "Erasmus, this no acceptance of our demands. This expressly states that all peoples — races, cultures, creeds — shall be viewed as equal in law. We cannot agree to that. It erodes our very way of life, and indeed, is the reason for us leaving our home in the first place."

"Mm?" Oom Erasmus blinked owl-like eyes of sleepiness. Maria bit her lip to prevent the smile spreading across her face. Poor man, the exertion of his communications had quite worn him out. "Oh, the conditions? Yes, they said we might not accept those. But a man is being sent up from Durban to tell us all about it. Tomorrow, they said."

His head nodded. A snore escaped from sagging lips.

Tannie Susanna rose from her chair, began pacing the floor. Her heels clicked on the flagstones.

"Maria, we must meet with this man tomorrow." She waved the page under Maria's nose. "I shall organise the womenfolk, take a delegation to his office and tell him what we think of the rules he intends to impose upon us."

Maria rested her embroidery in her lap, kept her eyes focussed on the neat stitches. "Should we not wait to hear what the details are first? Or leave it to the men, to the Council, to express the views of the community?"

Tannie Susanna wheeled around, her cheeks pink. Wisps of greying hair danced as she bobbed her head. "Wait? We cannot wait, Maria, dearest. We need to gain the upper hand, make our position on these matters clear. And as for leaving it for the men to intercede on our behalf — " a nod at her snoring husband, " — well, need I say more?"

Maria tested a giggle. Tannie Susanna flashed a smile in response.

"Maria, I must write letters, inform my friends we will present our case to this British envoy tomorrow afternoon." She settled back in her seat, pulled fresh notepaper towards her. "Would you be so good as to deliver them? This matter is too urgent for the regular postal service. I'll call you when I have them ready."

Maria clutched notes of reply from those she had delivered Tannie Susanna's instructions to, the errand taking far longer than anticipated. Her mind spun from the barrage of questions she couldn't answer; her stomach sloshed with offerings of tea while her hostess found paper and pen, composed a suitable response, and sent her on her way to repeat the process in the next house. And the next.

The winter sunset blazed in red and orange glory over the town as she hurried home. Lining the quiet streets, aloes bloomed in reflective splendour, transformed from the spiny tangle of summer to the magnificence of winter.

The recollection of another aloe, another day. Salve to heal a gaping wound. Maria's steps slowed. How long must she wait?

"Soon, Maria. We are not yet free from those who wish to chase us from this land. Only now it isn't Dingaan's tribe, but the British. They intend cutting us off from the port at Durban and have surrounded our people there. Commandant Pretorius has been summoned to their aid." A lift of the chin. Defying her expected complaint? "And I will ride with him."

The autumn buzz of insects, the lilting call of swallows preparing for their flight north, the lingering scents of summer. Their last meeting burned into her memory as the Tannie Johanne eyes lit with the excitement of battle.

Why would he sacrifice that up for her? Foolish to think, to hope, he would. No news, no visits all winter, despite the reported success of the mission. The notepaper crinkled between Maria's fingers as a spasm of realisation blew wisps of the old fog over the sunshine of her dream.

She waited in vain for Christiaan's return, didn't she?

CHAPTER TWENTY-TWO

Pietermaritzburg, South Africa. 5 August 1842

Tannie Susanna's white dress and hat gleamed against the dark wood panelling of the office. Sir Henry Cloete, rising from a desk too large for the room, extended a hand in welcome. His eyes darted to the group of women trailing in Tannie Susanna's wake.

"You have brought quite a delegation to our meeting, I see." Sir Henry's bushy eyebrows merged with his hairline. A neat beard, so unlike the wild, untamed examples of Maria's kinsmen, seemed to bristle with indignation. "I had anticipated one or two of you, but this is quite unexpected."

"Oh, this is nothing." Tannie Susanna wafted a hand at the twenty or so women crowding through the door. "There are another three hundred of us waiting outside. Isn't that so, Maria?"

Awed by her surroundings and the alarming flush of red in Sir Henry's cheeks, Maria could only nod in response.

"Well — " Sir Henry recovered his composure. "Take a seat, Mrs Smit. I'm afraid the rest of you will have to stand. Not enough chairs…"

"I'll stand, thank you."

"I shall sit." He did so, unbuttoning his stiff black jacket with one hand while pulling some papers towards him with the other. Next, he retrieved a pair of spectacles from a pocket, then perched them on his nose. He examined the papers without speaking.

Maria clenched her teeth against the impulse to fidget. Expecting to remain outside with the other women, she'd been surprised when Tannie Susanna had ushered her in alongside her inner circle. And honoured. Was her position at the house in Berg Street more than unpaid servant after all? A comforting thought amongst the many which swirled like leaves in the wind gusting up from the coast; at least she might expect a home in which to spend her declining spinster years.

Sir Henry cleared his throat. "Mrs Smit, you understand that I am here as special commissioner to Her Majesty's government and as such have been authorised to explain the conditions under which the British government has declared Natal its newest colony?" He paused, perhaps waiting for Tannie Susanna to respond. She remained silent. "Very well. We will hold meetings with your council, and trust for ratification of our terms with little debate. Lord Stanley, Secretary of State for War and the Colonies, has been more than fair in his agreeing to allow many of the institutions and systems you have in place to continue into the future."

He removed his spectacles, pinching the bridge of his nose between long, slender fingers.

"I see no particular reason for your petition today, Mrs Smit. Gratified though I am that you should wish to meet with me, I find there is little we have to discuss — "

"Little to discuss?" Maria blinked. She recognised that tone. Tannie Susanna ready to fight. "There is one major point to discuss, Sir Henry. And that is your government's condition that, and I quote — " a theatrical flourish of paper from her handbag. The same paper Oom Erasmus had given her the previous afternoon. "Now, where is it? Here. 'That there should not be in the eye of the law any distinction or disqualification whatever, founded on mere difference of colour, origin, language or creed'. Sir Henry, I do not believe you fully understand what you ask of us."

The chair squeaked as Sir Henry settled his weight. "Possibly I do not, Mrs Smit. I take it you care to enlighten me? I have five minutes." An exaggerated examination of the clock ticking in the corner.

Ticking away their freedom?

"Let me tell you what the last five years of my life has been like, Sir Henry. I left all I held dear; my home, my family, everything. In pursuit of one thing. The right to manage my affairs and my household in the way I deem fit, under the God in whom I believe and who I serve. I, together with my husband, with this young woman who sought refuge in our care — " Sir Henry turned his attention to Maria. If only the ground would open and swallow her whole. " — and with these women who gather before you, we packed up our lives and trekked over mountains, through deserts, across rivers, in search of a place where we could freely exercise this right."

"You have my admiration. And sympathies."

"I do not seek them, Sir Henry. I seek only to explain." Tannie Susanna sucked in a breath. "We have lost loved ones along the way."

The paper rustled, her tremble of grief threatening the self-control Maria knew she needed.

Lord, help her. If You're here.

"We have fought battles, and by the grace and promise of God, we have won. Against all odds, Sir Henry, we won. After all this, we arrived here, in this town. We established a settlement, safe, secure, and governed by the laws of the Lord. The Lord Almighty, Sir Henry, not your Queen." A crinkle of paper. "And now, you and your government believe it is for you to take that from us, to shackle us again with your earthly authority. It shall not be, Sir Henry."

The clock punctuated the sudden silence. Maria held her breath. At her side, Tannie Isobel reached for her hand with trembling fingers.

Sir Henry placed his spectacles on the desk. Spreading his palms over his papers, he pushed himself to his feet. The earlier pink flush darkened to the colour of a thundercloud. His eyebrows lowered and his nostrils flaring.

"You have said your piece, Mrs Smit." The quietness of his voice contrasted with the rage on his face, terrifying Maria more than any shouted insults. "I will present this offer to your council within the next three days. As it stands, with no alterations or changes. I fully expect them to agree. British order and rule — regardless of any supposed restrictions you feel we impose — can only be preferable to the near anarchy with which your current system of governance operates. The Natalia Republic experiment has failed, Mrs Smit. The sooner you realise it, the better."

Sir Henry returned to his chair, shuffled his papers together without another glance at Tannie Susanna and her ladies. A dismissal as effective as a door slammed in their faces.

"Sir, I would rather return across the Drakensberg barefoot than live as a subject under your British rule." Tannie Susanna gave a nod of farewell.

"Then I suggest you start walking, Mrs Smit. Please close the door on your way out."

CHAPTER TWENTY-THREE

Pietermaritzburg, South Africa. 8 August 1842

The lamp guttered in the draught from the open window. The curtains billowed, thick patterned fabric rustling and flapping. Maria stuffed a spare dress into her bag. What else should she pack? The mountains basked in crisp sunshine by day, but temperatures plummeted under the night-time shroud of dark shadows and frozen hollows. She shivered with remembrance. Her packing was inadequate, but it was all she felt able to carry. She would have to trust to the kindness of strangers, those who took regular pity on lone travellers wandering past their doors.

They won't welcome someone like you into their homes. The whisper mocked her naïve confidence.

Food. She nestled the parcel wrapped in sheets of paper on top of her dress. Dried meat, fruit, a few rusks.

A container of water. She could fill it as and when she found fresh water. Her recollections from the arduous journey under Piet Retief's leadership weren't as clear as she would have liked. Were there rivers and streams along the way, or had the oxen carried refreshment on their backs?

So long ago.

And all for what?

She tightened the fastenings of her bag. No more self-governing community of her people. No more Natalia Republic. Only Oom Erasmus, flush with the excitement of the day's discussions at the council, saluting their new masters with his suppertime wine. And Tannie Susanna, tight-lipped and wordless. Ladling the mutton stew into bowls, gravy dripping on the starched white tablecloth.

No mention of her threat to flee. No sending of Maria to gather the women in protest, to hitch up wagons or pack belongings.

Words. It was all words.

Words which ploughed the field of Maria's fragile comfort, tore up the precarious happiness of her settled life in this supposed promised land. Rekindled the desolation of farewell to Tannie Johanne. The collection of spring flowers on a graveside she should never have abandoned.

Maria pressed her hands to her mouth, silencing her pain before it could escape and make mischief in the quiet house.

Images rolled through her mind like the wheels of the wagons she'd come to detest. Tannie Margarite, entrusting her with the only piece of Ma she would ever possess. The clock now tucked under a protective layer of clothing, its pendulum removed and its marking of time silenced. The certainty it would become too cumbersome.

George. Teaching her to shoot, catching her when she fainted, teasing her as only a brother could.

Christiaan.

Always Christiaan.

No.

She'd only read of earthquakes in books, but the foundation of herself had shifted and tilted as it did in those pictures as Tannie Susanna recited her litany of hardships. Walls of promise, of hope and future, toppled and smashed to pieces with every recollected incident. Dreams tumbling as if the playthings of giants.

And then the ultimate betrayal. The declaration of resistance — of principled action against the unrighteous demands of a foreign invader defying the word of God — snoozing in the sitting room across the hallway, her knitting resting in her lap.

She'd been right. God had stayed in Graaff-Reinet, the companion of Tannie Johanne.

The embroidered sampler taunted her from its frame on the wall. Plans to prosper and not to harm? Nothing about her experiences bore that to be true. There were no plans, just a series of events forcing themselves upon her, crashing down and sweeping her away.

Still, it was her only connection with Tannie Johanne. Maria unclipped the frame, releasing the delicate cotton. She blinked against the scent of a far-distant home. Folding it into a careful square, she eased the gift into a pocket of her bag.

One final thing to do before gathering her shawl and slipping out into the darkening twilight.

Her fingers fumbled with the knot of leather, her nails snagging and tearing as she worked it loose. The carved wood fell to the floor. It could stay there.

She slung the straps of her bag over her shoulders, adjusting the weight until it balanced on her hips.

Toes curling at the cold of the flagstones, Maria crept to the front door. A shifting light flickered from the crack under the sitting room door. The sound of snoring. The smell of their evening meal. No movement.

Maria unlatched the door. Stepped over the threshold.

She left her boots on the step. So they would know.

CHAPTER TWENTY-FOUR

Pietermaritzburg, South Africa. 8 August 1842

Twilight darkened into evening. The moon hung in a purpling sky, lighting Maria's progress down the street. She winced at every sharp stone, stumbled at every corner.

Keep walking. One foot in front of the other. Have to get beyond the outskirts of town.

Once out of reach of any following search party, she would find a place to rest. Perhaps the outbuildings of a deserted farm. When would they notice her absence? At breakfast? Before? Only at lunchtime?

The clock pressed into the small of her back as she pushed onward. Past gardens of eerie-shadowed aloes and naked jacaranda trees awaiting their lilac-coloured summer gowns. A journey watched by sightless windows of shuttered cottages.

A dog barked.

Maria paused, held her breath, ears straining to discern the night noises. Was that the clink of a horse's bridle, the stamp of a hoof? No. Her wild imagination, nothing more.

Adjusting her burden, Maria resumed her pilgrimage, taking determined strides in preference to the halting, creeping steps of earlier. This was a matter of principle, keeping to Tannie Susanna's word, defying the British authorities and their ideas of power and rule. If she cut her feet to ribbons, collapsed on the path, slipped to her death in the jagged hostility of the mountains, so be it. At least she had seized control of her destiny, stopped waiting for the plans of others to favour and prosper her. For the plans of God.

Her life could count for something, the memory of her existence become a tale of courage and heroism told to the next generation of freedom-seekers. Of Voortrekkers.

Homes gave way to fields and farmland. The town's boundary stone crouched in white-washed encouragement — admonishment? — at the edge of the track.

Or she would die, lost and alone, her body broken and spirit shattered. No one mourning her passing. A load released from the shoulders of Oom Erasmus and Tannie Susanna. A line or two of regret from George. A shrug from Christiaan?

Her foot caught in a tree root straddling the path. Maria snatched at the air, desperate to catch herself from falling. The twigs of an overhanging bush scraped at her face, entangled her arms. She scrabbled for balance, but the bag shoved her to her knees.

Perhaps her path led to Pa's side, to Ma's caress? To an eternity without separation.

Or was that another fairy tale spun to comfort her grief?

The fog, her one constant companion from childhood, swept over her, thickening and billowing in a tempestuous storm. Powerless to overcome it, her resolve draining into paralysing numbness, Maria hugged her knees to her chest. Closed her eyes. Allowed the black rage to engulf her.

"Maria." A pinprick of light. A shaking. "Oh, Maria. What have you done?"

Done? Nothing. Leave me. So far to walk.

"Wake up, Maria. It's me. Christiaan."

Christiaan's voice, calling through the darkness.

No. Dreaming. Wishing. An animal whimper, scared, abandoned. Me.

"Lord, I need your help. Why did I delay? What foolish scheme of mine was more important than this? Than her?"

A weight blanketing her. Horse, wood-smoke. A coat?

Someone rubbing her hands. Rough fingers. Callouses. Tingling return to life. Struggling to the surface, to break free of the tendrils of despair, to open eyes glued with the crust of tears.

"Maria." A face hovering over hers. Shaggy curls. A wounded cheek.

Tannie Johanne eyes.

"You came." A croak. Who had her voice?

"Don't speak. Not yet. Let me help you sit up, get you warm first. Then we'll talk. All you like. For the rest of our lives."

Rest of our lives? Did he mean — ? Dizzy nausea as hands pulled her upright, draped woollen warmth over her shivering weakness.

"Let me light a fire. You need to get warm. Maria, what were you thinking? You could have died out here. Bandits, wild animals, the cold…"

"Not going back." Cracked lips. Cracked words. Cracked heart.

He mustn't have heard, busying himself with sticks and dried leaves and a flint from his pocket. One, two strikes. Sparks. Flames. Adding more firewood, stoking the blaze. Shoulders hunched. Did he talk to himself? To God?

Fire established, Christiaan at her side. "I'm going to move you closer. Can you wrap your arms around my neck? Good."

Lifted her like a child would her doll. Hugged her to his chest. His heartbeat thumping in her ear.

Propped her close to the fire. Her skin prickled. Heat thawed her body. Her heart? No fire could reach so deep.

"Are you comfortable? Can you sit unaided, just for a moment? I need my knapsack."

Chattering teeth and a half-nod.

He strode away towards a shape tethered to a tree. His horse. The clinking bridle. Not her imagination, after all.

He returned, bag in hand, shuffled next to her, encircling her with one arm while rummaging in the bag with the other.

"Tannie Susanna sent hot coffee. And bread. She said you left half your supper untouched. Thought you were sickening for something, especially when you retired early for bed instead of spending the evening with them as usual."

Tannie Susanna? What was he talking about?

A steaming mug pressed into her hands, his fingers wrapped around hers so she couldn't drop it. "Here, sip this. No, don't gulp, the shock will be too much."

Hot, sweet liquid moistened her lips, warmed her mouth, eased her constricted throat. Dribbled down her chin.

"Thank you." So she hadn't lost the ability to talk, then. She sipped again. "How are you here?"

Christiaan tightened his embrace, warmth seeping through his shirt. A candle flickered in her frozen heart.

"Where to begin? I heard about the decision of the council. I was close by. I'll explain that in a minute. Anyway, I guessed how you would all feel, Oom Erasmus and Tannie Susanna. And you." He paused, reaching to take the emptied cup. Kept his fingers entwined with hers. "I should have come sooner, Maria. I'm so sorry. I wanted everything perfect, before…I'm getting ahead of myself. I hurried to the house in Berg Street, but by the time I reached there, I feared I was too late. Everything seemed shut up for the night. But then I saw light under the curtain of the parlour window, so I knew someone remained awake. I hoped it would be you."

A thumb stroking her wrist.

"I tripped over your boots in the dark. I wondered why they were outside, when we've not had rain for days, but didn't think more of it until I was inside. Tannie Susanna went to call you from your room, saying she was certain you'd want to know of my visit, even if you were sick or sleeping. She returned in a fluster, bursting into the parlour and saying you weren't in your room, that your cupboard door was open, and your travelling bag was missing.

"She spoke in such a rush, Oom Erasmus and I were at a loss to understand her. But then the truth dawned on me. You'd run away. But how could that be right, your boots were on the step?

When I mentioned the fact, trying to reassure Tannie Susanna that you couldn't have gone far, she collapsed in a near faint in her chair.

"Once she'd recovered, she explained about your meeting with Sir Henry Cloete. And her response."

Christiaan shifted his position. threw another log onto the fire. Sparks danced, the wood popping and crackling in the stillness. Maria sucked in a shaking breath. A drowning man breaking the surface.

"When she handed me this — " he fumbled inside his shirt. A wooden cross on a length of leather string. Her necklace. " — I knew what you'd done. Will you ever forgive me, my dearest Maria?"

"Forgive you?" Maria's head whirled. It must be the coffee. Tannie Susanna must have added a touch of the brandy Oom Erasumus thought she didn't know about. "Whatever must I forgive you for? It's Tannie Susanna who betrayed her word. Not you…"

"But you thought I had, didn't you? That my promise to you meant nothing, that I wouldn't return as I told you God assured me I would." He turned her chin so his eyes searched hers. What did he read? The shattered wasteland of her broken heart? "For making plans without including you, asking you."

"Plans?"

"I've found a farm, Maria. On the edge of the mountains. It has a stream and a woodland and pasture perfect for horses. I've been negotiating — "

"That's wonderful, Christiaan." Maria struggled to free herself from the arm clamped around her shoulder, the hand cupping her chin. Did he hear the final blow of the hammer, the last remnants of herself disintegrating with every sentence he uttered? "I'm sure you'll make a wonderful farmer. I…I have to go. Must reach the mountains. Long night ahead. Before the weather turns. I — "

The fog rushed upon her, swallowed her in its malevolence. She doubled over, groaning and sobbing. Winded.

He waited for the turbulence to subside, rocking her and whispering as if calming a child.

"When we fought in Durban, the point of our offensive was to protect the port there. Shh, I'm not telling you a war story, I promise. It's a huge bay that curves inland for a mile or more. The worst of the weather is deflected by a bluff which marks the entrance to the harbour. Ships can shelter, re-provision, escape the storms.

"Early one morning — I had the first watch of the day — as dawn lit the horizon, a passage of the Psalms came to mind. I've memorised it since, holding it before the Lord as a prayer.

"I resigned from my post that same day. But I didn't want to come to you until everything was ready, until I could be certain my prayer was answered. It took me longer than I expected, and for that I am more than sorry. So many times I almost gave up, thought myself foolish to persist. And I missed you. With an ache I can't describe. But if I came to Pietermaritzburg, I knew I wouldn't be able to contain myself and would speak before I had anything of substance to offer."

"To offer? Christiaan, what — " Maria lifted her head, her pulse racing. Could summer follow winter so soon?

He placed a finger on her lips. "Wait. I haven't finished. The farm is now mine, Maria. When news of the council's decision reached me, I couldn't delay a moment longer. I saddled up my horse and rode as if the whole Zulu army chased me with their spears and venom." He chuckled, a ripple of life caressing Maria's skittering heart. "I came this evening to visit you, but also to put my request to Oom Erasmus and Tannie Susanna. As the closest you have to family here…"

The sun burst through the clouds in an explosion of joy. Christiaan held her fingers to his lips. The scar she'd help heal a jagged line of memory.

"Some went down to the sea in ships, doing business on the great waters; they saw the deeds of the Lord, his wondrous works in the deep. For he commanded, and raised the stormy wind, which lifted up the waves of the sea. Then they cried to the Lord in their trouble, and he delivered them from their distress; he made the storm be still, and the waves of the sea were hushed. Then they were glad because they had quiet, and he brought them to their desired haven. Let them thank the Lord for his steadfast love." The quote faded to a whisper. In the glow from the fire, Maria caught the glisten of tears. "I wish to be your desired haven, your safety from the storms. To shelter you in the quiet place of my love. Will you grant me that honour?"

The last of the fog evaporated. Voice for only one word. "Yes."

THE END

AUTHOR'S NOTE

The Great Trek took place in South Africa between 1835 and 1846. It was a movement of Dutch-speaking colonists from the Cape into the interior of southern Africa in search of land to establish their own homeland, independent of British rule.

These pioneers — voertrekkers in Dutch — had a strong Calvinist faith and came to believe their destiny was preordained by God as He led them into their promised land. These men and women became the founding fathers of the two Republics of the Free State and the Transvaal.

They travelled in ox-led wagons known as kakebeenwoens — literally, jawbone wagons — as the shape and sides resembled the jawbone of an animal. Too cumbersome to haul across the mountains the trekkers encountered en route, the wagons were dismantled on site, then reassembled once safely on the other side.

The key figures and events in MARIA's story are true. Gert Maritz led a party of voortrekkers from Graaff-Reinet, eventually joining Piet Retief in his endeavour to settle in the province of Natal.

Erasmus Smit was the unordained minister for the group and was married to Susanna Smit — Gert's sister. They had two sons, George and Salomon. Salomon died during the journey; George remained estranged from his mother until her death.

Gert Maritz died from ill-health while leading the settlement at Sooilaer in Natal.

Andries Pretorious became the new leader of the settlers in Natal. His 'victory commando' did battle against Zulu and British alike, with much success.

Sarel Cilliers was the unofficial pastor of the Great Trek, holding daily services and Sunday communion. At the behest of Andries Pretorious, he spoke the vow at which the trekkers promised to honour God throughout future generations should He give them victory over the Zulu king, Dingaan.

The Battle of Blood River took place one week later. Each year on 16 December, commemorations of The Day of the Covenant continued to be held by the Afrikaans community. In 1995, in the interests of nation building, President Nelson Mandela designated the holiday as The Day of Reconciliation.

Susanna Smit's encounter with Henry Cloete was the inspiration for MARIA's story. Although it is believed she declared her intention to return across the Drakensberg barefoot rather than endure British rule, she in fact never left Pietermaritzburg. I felt a principled young woman of MARIA's disposition would consider this something of a betrayal and so sent her on her barefoot way!

My apologies to those lovers and students of South African history for this potted version of perhaps one of the most significant events in the history of this country. I trust you enjoyed MARIA's personal story, as much as I enjoyed creating it.

Monument dedicated to Susanna Smit, the 'kaalvoutvrou'.

And now, please enjoy the first chapter of the next Prairie Rose Collection story, VIOLA by Kaitlene Dee

PRAIRIE ROSES COLLECTION

Sixth Annual

2024

ZOE BOOK 36 BY JANICE COLE HOPKINS

TRAVELING THE SANTA FE TRAIL AS A TUTOR, ZOE NEVER IMAGINED THE UNEXPECTED ADVENTURE OR THE HANDSOME ARMY OFFICER ESCORT SHE SO DISLIKED WOULD BE IN HER FUTURE.

EMMA BOOK 37 BY KAITLENE DEE

EMMA EXPECTED MORE ADVENTURE IN LIFE UNTIL HER FATHER, ON HIS DEATHBED, MARRIES HER OFF TO A MAN SHE BARELY KNOWS. WILL BUCK PUT OFF HIS OWN DREAMS?

PRAIRIE ROSES COLLECTION CONTINUED

SARAH Book 38 by Susan Horsnell

Sarah gives up on finding love and settles until her parents' death, debt, and injustice throw her life into chaos. Anthony,,is on his way to being a rancher, never guessing she could put that in jeopardy,

AILIS Book 39 by Michele Pollock Dalton

Struan is determined to find a place to call his own and joins the wagon train. A relative compels Ailis to undertake the treacherous journey that brings hard choices and sends her to her knees..

ENID Book 40 by Nancy Fraser

Fort Bridger being decommissioned forces Enid to either returning East with her parents or accept the opportunity of escorting a stranger to California. Simon is a clockmaker left in a lurch.

JANA Book 41 by Linda Carroll-Bradd

To protect her brother, Jana enters into a forced arrangemt of dangerous pretense with strangers. Rik, a bounty hunter on their trail, suspects the truth and wants to help, but will he go against his own standards?

PRAIRIE ROSES
COLLECTION CONTINUED

BETH Book 42 by Rena Groot
After the death of her parents, alone in the world, Beth believes her only course of action is a perilous journey West on the Oregon Trail. Unaware of the twists of fate that await, she journeys to an unimaginable destiny.

CHOLE Book 43 by Jennifer Branson
Tragedy forces Chloe to seek a new life. She decides to go west to Wyoming and encounters much more than she bargained for in an unwanted attraction to her handsome wagon master. Will she stay true to her faith?

MARIA Book 44 by Anna Jensen
A life of loss and sadness propels Maria to join the South African Voortrekkers in their search for freedom and land of their own. A ficticious account based on the story of a true Prairie Rose.

VIOLA Book 45 by Kaitlene Dee
Being widowed sets Viola free from a horrible husband, but she carries his baby. Rogan's best life awaits, preaching on Sundays and doctoring his flock through the week. He wants her to go with him. But will she?

PRAIRIE ROSES
COLLECTION CONTINUED

LUCY BOOK 46 BY ZINA ABBOTT

WHEN THE WAR LEAVES LUCY AND HER AUNT IN DIRE STRAIGHTS, THEY HEAD TO CALIFORNIA TO FIND HER ESTRANGED FATHER, BUT IT'S BEEN YEARS SINCE HE LEFT. MALACHI HESITATES ABOUT RETURNING TO THE EAST, BUT HIS GUT TELLS HIM TO GO AND PROTECT HIS FRIEND.

NORA BOOK 47 BY CARYL MCADOO

NORA HATES THE IDEA OF TRAVELING, MUCH LESS TO MARRY A STRANGER, BUT HER YOUNG COUSINS ARE DETERMINED. THOUGH THE JOURNEY CASTS DOUBTS ON GOD'S WILL, PASTOR JERICHO GETS THEM SAFELY TO WHERE THE MEN AWAIT. LET THE COURTING BEGIN!

DREA BOOK 48 BY KAREN GAMMONS

HER FATHER SELLS HIS BANK AND ANNOUNCES A MOVE FROM NEW YORK TO CALIFORNIA, TURNING DREA'S HIGH-SOCIETY WORLD UPSIDE DOWN. HIRING BROTHERS TO HELP THEM GET THERE DOES NOTHING TO EASE HER CONCERNS.

ENJOY THEM ALL!

VIOLA

© 2024 BY

KAITLENE DEE

Linley Valley, California – Spring, 1865

For the hundredth time since she was married, Viola Stanford Lee stood at the bedroom window of her small home watching the sun rise over the mountains to the east. Once again, she wondered if she should pack her things and run away from her husband, Allen Lee.

She'd thought to shoot her husband, but the blacksmith's wife, Kay, who was teaching her to sew and about living a life pleasing to the Lord, heavily discouraged it. Which was too bad; Allen lived his life half-dead anyway. Why Pa had sent her to *this man* for life, she hadn't a clue. Like Allen, Pa was drunk most of the time and probably thought he was doing what was best by both Viola and Emma. Pa had a small and struggling farm to work, and when they lost Mama, it was all he could do to get out of bed every morning and not reach for the bottle.

Still, she could have helped. Gotten a job and contributed to the family's welfare. Anything would've been better than the cold heart of Allen.

Allen Lee…he was a miner with a sack full of gold dust that he spent before it ever hit his pockets. Many times, he would come home smelling of cheap perfume and whiskey. Often, she was forever grateful for the booze he'd guzzled because it meant he staggered in through the doorway of their home and passed out on the sofa. Only once, about a month and a half ago, had he pressed for her to fulfill her wifely obligations.

She pushed the thought away; he had actually tried to court her that evening with flowers and compliments on dinner. Never praise about her, though. She was always an afterthought for him. There were times the cupboards were practically bare, and she went without, while he sipped glass after glass of whatever amber liquid the saloons were serving. He gambled away whatever he'd earned doing who-knows-what. His life was his to live as he pleased, he'd often told her, and hers was to serve him and keep the house clean. It set her teeth on edge; toward him for treating her that way, and in regards to her father for marrying her to this scoundrel.

I don't think I can survive a lifetime of this. Lord, help me to make it through today, please.

A knock at the door startled Viola from her musings and half felt prayer. She still hadn't ruled out shooting Allen as being completely absurd. She shook her head. *What am I thinking, Lord?*

She scurried to the small parlor and opened the door, hoping it wouldn't be Allen too drunk to work the doorknob. Relief sprung through her to see it was her sister, Emma, along with her new husband, Buck.

Emma launched herself into Viola's arms. "Vi, I can't believe it! I know I saw you yesterday," her sister's voice quivered, "but when I woke this morning, I was afraid I'd dreamed finding you dead!"

They released one another from a tight hug, but still held hands as Viola looked over her sister.

Buck cleared his throat, bringing awareness to the two sisters that he was still there. He held up a basket. "We brought sustenance."

Viola invited them in, hoping Allen wouldn't show up, toss them out in nothing less than his usual rude fashion, and demand her to make him breakfast. Truth be told, she had nothing in the house but a small sack of corn meal, a few tablespoons of saleratus, an egg, a bit of lard, and a half bowl of unground coffee beans. Her stomach hadn't growled yet, but hunger was coming on now that the aromas from the basket hit her senses.

Viola showed her sister and brother-in-law into the kitchen. Buck kindly took a wooden chair from the living room and brought it in so they could all be seated, as there were only two chairs at the table.

Sitting at the table with wonder in her heart, Viola stared at her sister, and asked her to share more about their journey to Linley Valley. She still couldn't believe that her baby sister— five years younger than herself—had married and was now sitting right here in front of her! *Lord, please let theirs be a love match.*

She pulled herself from her desperate prayers for her sister and Buck. He seemed nice, like a good, good man, and attentive to Emma.

Deep within, Viola prayed Buck was all the things to her sister that he seemed in this moment. All the things Allen was not; had never been, and likely will never be. To Allen, she was nothing but a servant.

"We brought fresh blueberry muffins from the restaurant," Emma said. "Sliced apples, cheese, a tin of tea, and several slices of crispy bacon."

"I'll put on some water for the tea," Viola stood, then stirred the coals and added some wood to the stove and put the kettle on. As hungry as she was now, and as much as she wanted to visit with her sister and new brother-in-law, Viola's stomach churned at the thought of Allen coming home to find they had guests. He would not like that another man was in his house, uninvited by him. It didn't matter that it was her sister's husband. For that matter, Allen wouldn't like her sister being there without first seeking his permission for visitors.

When he had presented himself to her Pa, he did so as a decent man, but it was all an act to gain a new widower's confidence. Allen's success in gold mining hadn't been a part of the deception. He was successful finding the shiny metal, but he was unsuccessful at saving it. He spent it on a highfalutin' time while she lived in squalor.

Now her Pa was gone. She didn't know how to quell the anger she had toward him for binding her to Allen for a lifetime. She didn't want to admit it, but she didn't think she could forgive God for this imprisonment to a life she didn't want.

Kay Bentley, her best friend—only friend—in Linley Valley, assured her that we're God's handiwork, created in Christ Jesus for good works, which He prepared beforehand, and that we should walk in them. How could this be true when her husband kept her at home most of the time? Nothing made sense about life and how things work out, especially for her.

Viola turned back to the table.

Emma had found the only two plates and mugs in the house and set one for her and Buck to share and a plate and mug for Viola.

Shame over her living conditions crept up in Viola, but she focused on her sister and how Buck doted on Emma. They seemed truly happy. This brought some joy into Viola's heart.

The water in the kettle was warmed enough, so Viola poured it into their cups, which already had tea leaves in a strainer sitting over top of the cups' rims.

After Viola had taken her seat again, Buck prayed over the food.

After prayer, Viola considered how she might politely get rid of them. She really needed for them to leave—and soon! She couldn't risk them being there when Allen returned, but there was so much she wanted to know about their journey here, how Pa had passed away, and what had happened to their farm.

"Viola?" Buck was studying her intently.

"Yes?" She felt like a timid mouse, ready to flee a dangerous situation—did she look that way too?

"Is something wrong? You're shaking," Emma set her mug down, her face drawn in deep concern as she stared at Viola.

Swallowing the bite of muffin she'd just taken, Viola looked from her sister to her brother-in-law, before dropping her gaze to her lap. "Allen could be walking through the door at any time now. He won't like it that you're here—he's jealous. He won't like it that you brought food, it would wound his pride."

Emma looked stricken. "What should we do? You need to eat. I knew from our brief visit yesterday that you didn't have much in the house. Please, eat and then we'll make short work of cleaning up and take everything with us."

Buck shifted in his seat. He clearly didn't like what he'd heard, and maybe what he saw—or lack thereof, but he remained silent, thoughtful but silent.

A terse knock at the door alarmed all three of them.

Somehow, Buck seemed to sit taller and took on a protective demeanor.

Viola didn't want a confrontation between Buck and Allen. There was no telling how far Allen would escalate things.

Someone rapped at the door again, only louder. "Mrs Lee, it's deputy Finley," the deputy called in from the parlor door.

Viola looked to her sister as she stood and rushed to the door, Emma and Buck in tow.

She pulled open the door to see the deputy whip his hat off. "Please come in."

"I'm right sorry to bother you, ma'am, and right sorry to bring you bad news." He noticed Buck and Emma and gave a quick nod in their direction. "Maybe we should discuss this in another room?"

Viola turned to her sister before introducing Buck and Emma to the deputy.

"Well, seeing as they're family, I'm sorry to tell you that Mr Lee has been shot. He didn't survive."

Viola's jaw dropped as her knees buckled beneath her.

Thankfully, Buck caught her, swept her up, then set her on the sofa.

Viola tried to lay hold of what had just been said, but she just couldn't believe it. Her husband, Allen Lee, was dead.

PREVIOUS PRAIRIE ROSES COLLECTIONS

2020 PRAIRIE ROSES COLLECTION
2ND ANNUAL COLLECTION

Lilah
CARYL MCADOO

Susan
PATRICIA PACJAC CARROLL

Kate
DONNA SCHLACHTER

STRONG HEROINES TRAVELING WEST IN COVERED WAGONS!

THE LORD IS HIGH & LIFTED UP!

PRAIRIE ROSES COLLECTION THREE
2021

Ruth
CARYL MCADOO

Cadi
LINDA CARROLL-BRADD

Tess
ANNEE JONES

Sophie
PATRICIA PACJAC CARROLL

WAGON HO!

COVERED WAGON HEROINES!

YOU WILL NOT WANT TO MISS THESE AWESOME STORIES!

Ella

NANCY FRASER

Calli

DONNA SCHLACHTER

Laney

VICKIE McDONOUGH

Sabra

PATRICIA PACJAC CARROLL

2022 COLLECTION

Pearl

ZINA ABBOTT

Glory

MARISA MASTERSON

Rose

RENA GROOT

Aria

SHONDA ZESCHIN FISCHER

Elsie

KC HART

Amity

LINDA CARROLL-BRADD

Amy

ANGELA LAIN

Jo

CARYL McADOO

 All the Prairie Roses authors hope you enjoy all the stories of our collection and that you'll bless them with a quick review posted around your social media (Facebook, Twitter, Instagram, ect.) as well as at Amazon, GoodReads, BookBub, AllAuthor, and your blog!

It's easiest to do while the story is fresh on your mind, and there's no need for a long, drawn-out synopsis. Even authors hate writing those! ☺ Just a few of your own words telling why you liked it works great. Maybe you might mention a favorite character or scene. Make it easy on yourself!

THANK YOU SO MUCH ahead of time!

Read all the Prairie Roses' stories:

Prairie Roses Collection One: - 2019

    SADIE by Patricia PACJAC Carroll   book one

    REMI by Caryl McAdoo   book two

    HOPE by Barbara Goss   book three

    JULIA by Vickie McDonough   book four

Prairie Roses Collection Two - 2020

    LILAH by Caryl McAdoo   book five

    SUSAN by Patricia PACJAC Carroll   book six

    KATE by Donna Schlachter   book seven

Prairie Roses Collection Three - 2021

    RUTH by Caryl McAdoo   book eight

    TESS by Annee Jones   book nine

    SOPHIE by Patricia PACJAC Carroll   book ten

    CADI by Linda Carroll-Bradd   book eleven

Prairie Roses Collection Four – 2022

    ELLA by Nancy Fraser   book twelve

    CALLI by Donne Schlachter   book thirteen

    LANEY by Vickie McDonough   book fourteen

    SABRA by Patricia PACJAC Carroll   book fifteen

    PEARL by Zina Abbott   book sixteen

    GLORY by Marisa Masterson   book seventeen

ROSE by Rena Groot	book eighteen
ARIA by Shonda Fischer	book nineteen
ELSIE by KC Hart	book twenty
AMITY by Linda Carroll-Bradd	book twenty-one
AMY by Angela Lain	book twenty-two
JO by Caryl McAdoo	book twenty-three

Prairie Roses Collection Four – 2023

STELLA by Patricia PacJac Carroll	book twenty-four
CLARA by Zina Abbott	book twenty-five
EMILY by Nancy Fraser	book twenty-six
ANNE by Rena Groot	book twenty-seven
IZZY by Caleb Gammons	book twenty-eight
TINA by Donna Schlachter	book twenty-nine
HELEN by Elissa Strati	book thirty
TILDA by Linda Carroll-Bradd	book thirty-one
IVY by Joi Copeland	book thirty-two
GRACE by Kaitlene Dee	book thirty-three
AVA by Caryl McAdoo	book thirty-four
BEE by Karen Gammons	book thirty-five

Prairie Roses Collection Five – 2024

ZOE by Janice Cole Hopkins	book thirty-six
EMMA by Kaitlene Dee	book thirty-seven
SARAH by Susan Horsnell	book thirty-eight
AILIS by Michele Pollock Dalton	book thirty-nine

About the Author

I'm a British expat who has lived in South Africa for a little over twenty years. My husband and I live with our two teenage children on the east coast, a few miles north of the city of Durban. We overlook the Indian Ocean where we have the privilege of watching dolphins and whales at play.

My first book *The Outskirts of His Glory* was published in May 2019. The book is a Christian devotional and poetry collection, exploring the many surprising ways that God can speak to us through His creation. I have drawn on my travels in and around South Africa, as well as further afield, to hopefully inspire each of us to slow down and perhaps listen more carefully to the 'whispers of His ways' (Job 26:14) that are all around us.

Since publishing *Outskirts*, I have had the privilege of speaking at a number of local churches and even have a weekly slot on a Christian radio station. I have also continued writing by contributing to a variety of blogs and online writing communities as well as developing my own website and blog.

Want to know more? Check out my website at
www.annajensen.co.uk

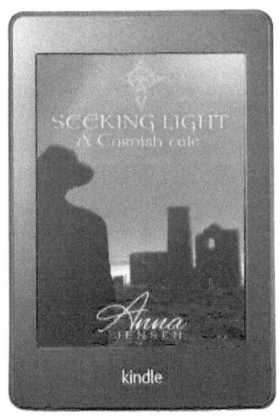

Cornwall, September 1742

*Tin mining is in Jem Pearce's blood. For as long as he can
remember, the subterranean caverns of the Cornish mines have
been his world — just like his father before him. Intimate
knowledge of the maze of tunnels and passageways lights the
way in the underground darkness, as sure as any lantern.*

*So why, when mine owner Mr Roberts announces plans for a
proposed expansion project, is Jem so uneasy?*

*Compounding his anxiety is his son Edward's eagerness to
experience the thrill of the blasting preparations.*

*Can Jem persuade the mine officials to change their plans, and
so avert disaster?*

*Meanwhile, Mr John Wesley has returned to this remote part of
the country with his vibrant Gospel crusades. Thousands gather
to hear his simple, hope-filled teaching, including Susanna*

Pearce, Jem's wife. Can she help her husband discover the true light that shines in the deepest darkness — the light that is Jesus?

Make it easier to hear about all things Anna and sign up for my free more-or-less monthly newsletter. You'll receive a gift of the ebook, Seeking Light, a Cornish tale inspired by my years living in Cornwall when you do. You'll also be sent an invitation to join my Subscriber Family Birthday Club. Sign up today at www.annajensen.co.uk/news

Follow me across my various social media platforms. Or email me directly at hello@annajensen.co.za I'd love to connect with you.

The Ripples Through Time

Ripples Through Time is a series of novels telling stories of the past and showing how they inspire our present. Stories of how God takes the ordinary and transforms it into something extraordinary. The smallest of stones, tossed into smooth water, will create waves; concentric circles spreading outward to reach beyond the immediate or seen. So too, the seemingly insignificant actions of today can leave ripples that are felt into eternity.

There is the village of Eyam and her inhabitants' love and sacrifice which saved a generation, the Bletchley Park codebreakers' dedication to fight a war far from public praise, the adventure and ingenuity of diamond hunters settling in the impermanence of the Namibian desert, and the discovery of a 2000-year-old fishing vessel believed to date to the time of Jesus and his disciples. Campaigns and conflicts, castles and cottages – tales to uncover and histories to unfold.

These are the pebbles and the ripples they leave.

The *Ripples Through Time* series is dedicated to my personal mentor, author Marion Ueckermann, who sadly passed away on 25 June 2021. She included a devotion entitled *Reflections in Pebbles* in the multi-author boxed set, *In All Things* (a set which I also contributed to). I would like to leave you with this quote from Marion:

'God has chosen you to be His pebble in the sea of humanity. What ripples of hope could emit from the splashes of your life? What giants could tumble from the impact of one small stone, one random act of kindness?'

May you, like Marion, become a pebble in the hand of God, leaving ripples in the world as you pass.

Remembered Lives
where the past and present collide

From the back cover

Are not two sparrows sold for a penny? And not one of them will fall to the ground apart from your Father. But even the hairs of your head are all numbered. Fear not, therefore; you are of more value than many sparrows.

Anfield Stadium, Liverpool, England. Home ground of the Liverpool Football Club. And place of remembrance for the 96 victims of one of the worst football disasters in British history.

South Africa, 1899-1900. A bitter war rages between Britain and the Boer republics of the Transvaal and the Free State. Boer commandoes lay siege to towns in British-controlled Natal. The British Army must fight to relieve them.
But first they must reach them, marching into hostile terrain against an enemy with unrivalled marksmanship skills, and travelling on horseback.

Both sides target Spionkop, a hill rising from the Natal plains - destined to be christened 'an acre of massacre' by watching reporter, Winston Churchill; and to find its name gracing one of the most famous football stands in the world; Anfield's The Kop.

South Africa, 2015. Liverpool football fans Jimmy, Sarah, and Des travel to South Africa to commemorate the Hillsborough Disaster, where they discover more than they expect - about the distant past, and about themselves.

Scan the QR code to order your copy of Remembered Lives.
Free in Kindle Unlimited.

Given Lives

A Village. A Plague. An extraordinary love.

SEPTEMBER 1665.

Plague ravages the English capital, London. Thousands are left dead.

In the Derbyshire village of Eyam, 160 miles north of the London tragedies, Kitty Allenby is settling into country life. Encouraged by her Aunt Anne and Uncle Robert, she is excited for the year ahead.

That is until a stranger arrives from London, bringing a parcel of cloth for the local tailor – cloth infested with plague-carrying fleas.

Within weeks, Eyam is under siege.

By spring 1666, drastic action is needed to contain the spread of disease. What can be done?

The Reverend William Mompesson thinks he knows. For his plan to succeed, Mompesson will need the co-operation of the whole community, including his predecessor and rival, Thomas Stanley.

Will the two men be able to put aside the deep mistrust of one another for the sake of the people they are called to serve? How will the doomed villagers respond?

And what of Kitty? Can she learn to love a community not her own, perhaps paying the ultimate price alongside strangers she barely knows?

Based on true events, Given Lives is a story of bravery and sacrifice, of love that laid itself down for the sake of others. It is a whisper through time to each of us confronted by a modern plague, the global Covid 19 pandemic. Will we attune our ears and listen?

'My great aunt (nine times over) and ancestor, Margaret Blackwell, is part of this wonderful novel and, as a family survivor of this dreadful plague, I felt privileged to be asked to read Anna's novel.

The story unfolds as Kitty comes to Eyam to celebrate the annual Wakes Week and becomes isolated with the villagers as they try to contain the disease. It captures the real depth of sacrificial love, care and compassion and their heroism during the plague outbreak in 1665–66. The trust and hope the families had in God to bring them through this tragic time is a real testament to their fortitude, as Kitty constantly, with her family, looks forward to a brighter and happier future.

It's a great read. and my thanks to Anna for her factual insight and passion for our history.' — Joan Plant, Descendant of a Plague Survivor

Scan the QR code to order your copy of Given Lives. Free in Kindle Unlimited.

Secret Lives

Two Women. Two Generations. One World War.

Can you keep a secret?

February 1942

Alice Stallard, encouraged by her two friends, submits her entry to the Daily Telegraph prize crossword – a crossword she solves in record time. She thinks nothing more about it until called into the study of her Cambridge University professor where she's invited to an interview at the mysterious Bletchley Park near Bedford.

Once at Bletchley Park, Alice is confronted with the Official Secrets Act and months of training for a job no one will talk about. After being moved from one training centre to another, her final posting is to Station 53a of the Special Operations Executive – Winston Churchill's 'Ministry of Ungentlemanly Warfare'.

But what of when the War is over? Will Alice keep her promise of silence?

February 1998

A-levels loom on the horizon for 18-year old Rosie Mason. She had expected her favourite subject to be History but instead is finding it dull and lifeless. Perhaps the drama and romance she was hoping for can be found elsewhere – in her grandmother's memories. But Gran is reluctant to share any war stories, changing the subject at every one of Rosie's questions.

Determined to conquer Gran's reticence, Rosie decides to spend her long post-exam holiday with her grandparents. After days of trying, Gran agrees to show Rosie a few photos -- and the first edition copy of C S Lewis' The Screwtape Letters.

Only when Rosie stumbles on a handwritten note tucked between the pages of Screwtape does the silence of decades threaten to unravel.

Scan the QR code to order your copy of Secret Lives. Free in Kindle Unlimited.

Our House on Sycamore Street

Our House on Sycamore Street is a new multi-author, multi-genre series set in quaint and quirky Eden Cove, an English seaside town with plenty of spirit. With stories of redemption and salvation behind every door, you're sure to find a new tale of romance, intrigue, humour or heart. All you have to do is knock!

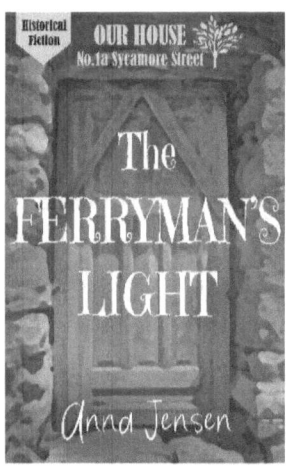

The Ferryman's Light

He has plans for the future. What happens when circumstances dictate those plans must change?

If you love an historical origins drama, you'll be sure to enjoy The Ferryman's Light

October, 1853: Walter Ferryman's life is simple and predictable, running the Eden Cove ferry while his father works as gamekeeper to Castle on the Hill owners, the Wingfields.

That is until sweetheart Susan Wingfield reveals a dreadful secret - which puts all Walter's future hopes and plans into jeopardy. Will Walter find the courage to own his mistakes? How will he make good on his promise to Susan while remaining in Eden Cove?

Buy now from Amazon or scan the QR code

Welcome to Our House on Sycamore Street

Our House on Sycamore Street is a new multi-author, multi-genre series set in quaint and quirky Eden Cove, an English seaside town with plenty of spirit. With stories of redemption and salvation behind every door, you're sure to find a new tale of romance, intrigue, humour or heart. All you have to do is knock!

Other books can be read in any order:

The Italian Musician's Sanctuary by Danielle Grandinetti

The Outsider's Welcome by Vida Li Sik

The Daughter's Truth by Claire Lagerwall

The Light Keeper's Wife by Jennifer Mistmorgan

The Key Collector's Promise by Donna Jo Stone

The Maestro's Missing Melody by Amy Walsh

The Niece's Aussie Patient by Meredith Resce

The Runaway's Redemption by Allyson Koekhoven

The Bookbinder's Daughter by Lynn Dean

The Widow's Request by Ashley Winter

The Lost Daughter's Irishman by Carolyn Miller

The Mother's Song by Caroline Johnston

The Wedding Planner's Predicament by Dianne J. Wilson

OUR HOUSE on Sycamore Street

BOOK 1: THE FERRYMAN'S LIGHT   *by Anna Jensen*

He has plans for the future. What happens when circumstances dictate those plans must change?

BOOK 2: THE ITALIAN MUSICIAN'S SANCTUARY

by Danielle Grandinetti

Hunted by one man, can she open her heart to another?

BOOK 3: THE OUTSIDER'S WELCOME

by Vida Li Sik

If you love women's fiction, you will enjoy The Outsider's Welcome, a tale of resilience, community, and a search for belonging.

BOOK 4: THE DAUGHTER'S TRUTH   *by Claire Lagerwall*

Emmy Whitehouse is about to discover that everything she knows is not at all what she thinks.

BOOK 12: THE LOST DAUGHTER'S IRISHMAN
by Carolyn Miller

She wants to find a way to live again; he wants to close a deal and move on. Until sparks fly and these opposites attract in this contemporary romance filled with heart and humour.

BOOK 13: THE MOTHER'S SONG   *by Caroline Johnston*

Miranda McVitty, wife, mother and campsite owner. Miranda loves to sing as she goes about her work and this summer she's learning to sing her prayers as well as her to do list.

BOOK 14: THE WEDDING PLANNER'S PREDICAMENT
by Dianne J. Wilson

Cleo is done organizing weddings. James has a wedding to plan, and Cleo is his only hope.

St Saviours Seasonal Stories

The seasons of the church calendar are important to Richard, vicar of St Saviours, a thriving church community in the heart of London. Christmas, Easter, Advent and Lent — all have a special place in the Reverend's heart and actions.

A Candle for Christmas
Four candles. Four stories. One Christmas Day.

The vicar of St Saviour's is preparing for Christmas. Four Sundays, four services, four advent candles to light.

Richard loves Christmas. And he loves the ritual of the advent candles. Only this year is different. Memories and regrets threaten to spoil his favourite season.

Joelle is tired. Tired of the streets; tired of the weather. Tired of being unseen. Could the preparations for Christmas at St Saviour's herald a new beginning?

Tamara knows this Christmas is going to be different. She's been planning for weeks. But will it be in the way she expects or is there a surprise in store?

Ellen realises her new-found freedom isn't as wonderful as she expected it to be. Can she retrace her steps and find restoration? Or is it too late?

Christmas Day. Richard ignites the final candle…

The Nine Readings of Christmas
Nine lessons. One Christmas story

Christmas is fast approaching.

The congregation of St Saviours is caught up with Christmas preparations and parties — not least amongst them their vicar, Richard.

The service of Nine Lessons and Carols has been months in the planning. Everything is in place for the evening to be the highlight of this year's church calendar. Until Richard receives a telephone call; his soloist has a sore throat. Can The Service still go ahead? Will Richard seek to find his own solution? Or will God have His way?

Marjorie is baking up a storm; containers full of every Christmas treat occupying all available space. When a Christmas card from afar arrives with unwelcome news — and a gift — Marj is forced to reassess the life she has chosen. Is she where she should be or has her focus on family and church been misdirected?

Ellen, studying and involving herself in the local community, is experiencing dreams of Africa. What do they mean? And does an email she receives have anything to do with them?

Tamara has made her peace with the single life she now leads. But is there more? Are a young girl, a homeless woman, and a Christmas party the key to her happiness?

Joelle has a new home, with a comfortable bed and two cooked meals a day. She also has a family — the family of St Saviours. Can she help Ellen decipher her dreams and discover her heart? Or show Tamara that they are more alike than she may think? Christmas at St Saviours. Nine lessons; one story.

One Passing Easter
Seven special days. And the lives they changed

Shrove Tuesday. The annual St Saviours Pancake Relay is in full flip. Runners and spectators alike are wild with excitement. Until an accident occurs and an ambulance is called. Reverend Richard has a full schedule of services and events planned between now and Easter Sunday. Will he be able to continue as arranged, or will circumstances dictate otherwise?

Tamara, persuaded to go on a blind date by a friend and colleague, is desperate for change. Abandoning the shallowness of yet another meaningless relationship, she seeks something deeper this Lent. Can she find the love she longs for? Or will past experiences and hurts keep her in their grip?

Joelle harbours a secret. Does she have the courage to share it with Marjorie? Or is time running out?

Elsewhere, Ellen has found her calling. Or so she hopes. But when disaster strikes her community, bringing with it an unexpected confrontation, can beauty rise from the ashes? After this one passing Easter, the lives of the St Saviours community may never be the same.

Also available as an eBook three-in-one box set.

The St Saviours Seasonal Stories: The Collection.

Scan the QR code for the St Saviours Seasonal Stories series page on Amazon. All titles are FREE in Kindle Unlimited

www.ingramcontent.com/pod-product-compliance
Lightning Source LLC
Chambersburg PA
CBHW021154130626
46554CB00005B/1819